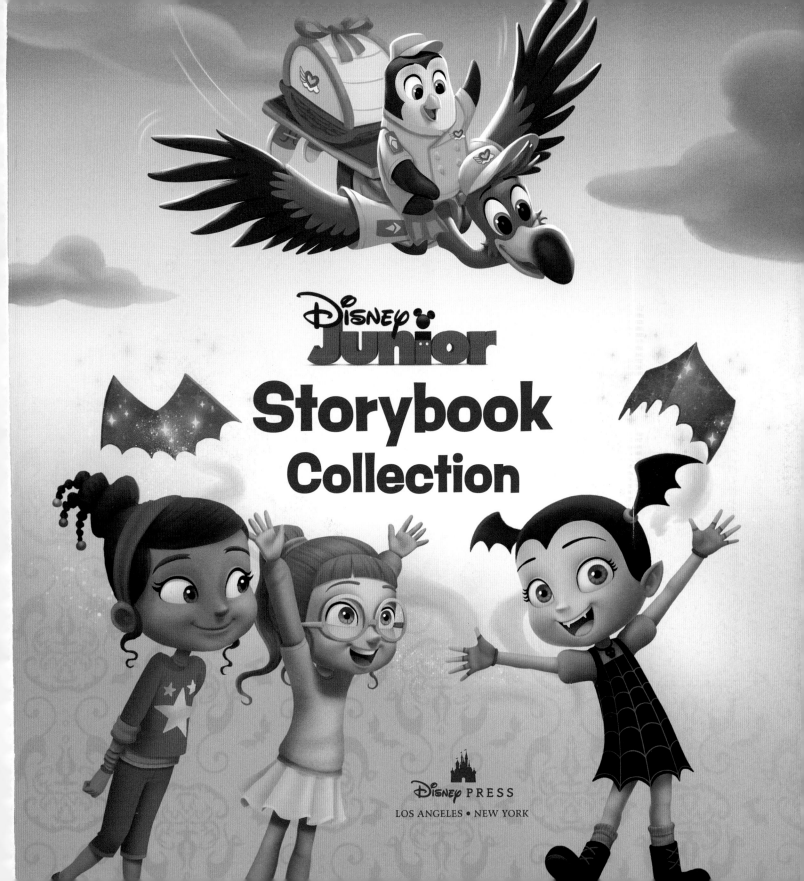

Disney Junior

Storybook Collection

Disney PRESS

LOS ANGELES • NEW YORK

Contents

Mira, Royal Detective
Meet Mira 1

T.O.T.S.
Bunny Bunanza 19

Mickey Mouse Clubhouse
Super Adventure 35

Vampirina
Vee's Monster Bash 53

Doc McStuffins
Head Nurse Hallie 69

Elena of Avalor
Song of the Sirenas 87

Puppy Dog Pals
The Last Pup-icorn 103

Minnie
A Walk in the Park 121

Mira, Royal Detective
Undercover Princess 139

Meet Mira! Queen Shanti chose her to be the royal detective of the kingdom of Jalpur. Before Mira, all the royal detectives were grown-ups. Mira may be small, but she's mighty!

Meet Mira

"Meet Mira" written by Sascha Paladino. Copyright © 2020 Disney Enterprises, Inc.

"Bunny Bunanza" adapted by Becky Friedman. Based on the episode written by Amy Keating Rogers. Copyright © 2020 Disney Enterprises, Inc.

"Super Adventure" adapted by Bill Scollon. Based on the episode written by Mark Seindenberg. Copyright © 2013 Disney Enterprises, Inc.

"Vee's Monster Bash" adapted by Chelsea Beyl. Based on the episode "Hauntleyween," written by Travis Braun. Copyright © 2018 Disney Enterprises, Inc.

"Head Nurse Hallie" adapted by Annie Auerbach. Based on the episode "Made to Be a Nurse," written by Chelsea Beyl for the series created by Chris Nee. Copyright © 2017 Disney Enterprises, Inc.

"Song of the Sirenas" adapted by Rachel Ruderman. Based on the episode written by Sylvia Olivas and Rachel Ruderman for the series created by Craig Gerber. Copyright © 2018 Disney Enterprises, Inc.

"The Last Pup-icorn" adapted by Sheila Sweeny Higginson. Based on the episode written by Jean Ansolabehere for the series created by Harland Williams. Copyright © 2020 Disney Enterprises, Inc.

"A Walk in the Park" adapted by Gina Gold. Based on the episode written by Jennifer Heftler. Copyright © 2014 Disney Enterprises, Inc.

"Undercover Princess" adapted by Sascha Paladino. Based on the episode written by Amy Keating Rogers. Copyright © 2020 Disney Enterprises, Inc.

"Hawaii Pug-O" adapted by Michael Olson. Based on the episode written by Bob Smiley for the series created by Harland Williams. Copyright © 2017 Disney Enterprises, Inc.

"Realm of the Jaquins" adapted by Tom Rogers. Based on the episode written by Sylvia Olivas and Craig Gerber. Copyright © 2017 Disney Enterprises, Inc.

"Mickey and Donald Have a Farm" written by Bill Scollon. Based on the episode written by Mark Seindenberg. Copyright © 2012 Disney Enterprises, Inc.

"Smitten with a Kitten" adapted by Kerri Grank. Based on the episode written by Shea Fontana for the series created by Chris Nee. Copyright © 2016 Disney Enterprises, Inc.

"Panda Excess" adapted by Travis Braun. Based on the episode written by Amy Keating Rogers. Copyright © 2019 Disney Enterprises, Inc.

"Vampire for President" adapted by Nancy Parent. Based on the episode written by Chelsea Beyl. Copyright © 2020 Disney Enterprises, Inc.

"Hocus-*Bow*-cus" written by Gina Gold. Copyright © 2014 Disney Enterprises, Inc.

"Adopt-a-Palooza" adapted by Sheila Sweeny Higginson. Based on the episode written by Jessica Carleton for the series created by Harland Williams. Copyright © 2019 Disney Enterprises, Inc.

"Space Adventure" written by Susan Amerikaner. Copyright © 2011 Disney Enterprises, Inc.

All illustrations by the Disney Storybook Art Team

Published by Disney Press, an imprint of Buena Vista Books, Inc. No part of this book may be reproduced or transmitted in any form or by any means, electronic or mechanical, including photocopying, recording, or by any information storage and retrieval system, without written permission from the publisher.

For information address Disney Press, 1200 Grand Central Avenue, Glendale, California 91201.

Printed in the United States of America

First Hardcover Edition, September 2021

Library of Congress Control Number: 2021932738

10 9 8 7 6 5 4 3 2 1

ISBN 978-1-368-06583-2

FAC-038091-21225

For more Disney Press fun, visit www.disneybooks.com

SUSTAINABLE FORESTRY INITIATIVE — Certified Sourcing
www.sfiprogram.org
SFI-01268
This Label Applies to Text Stock Only

Puppy Dog Pals
Hawaii Pug-O 157

Elena of Avalor
Realm of the Jaquins 173

Mickey Mouse Clubhouse
Mickey and Donald Have a Farm 189

Doc McStuffins
Smitten with a Kitten 203

T.O.T.S.
Panda Excess 219

Vampirina
Vampire for President 235

Minnie
Hocus-*Bow*-cus 253

Puppy Dog Pals
Adopt-a-Palooza 269

Mickey Mouse Clubhouse
Space Adventure 285

Mira's friends Mikku and Chikku are mongooses. They join her on all her cases, but they often get distracted by snacks.

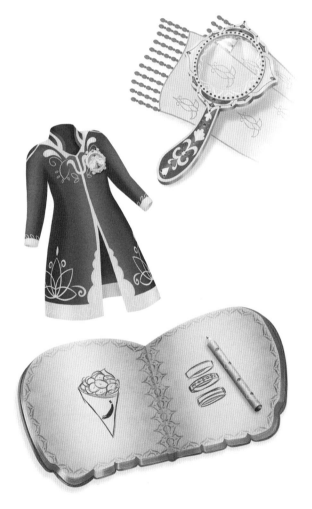

Like all royal detectives before her, Mira has some special things to help her solve mysteries. Her jacket and badge tell everyone that she's a detective. Her magnifying glass helps her look closely at things. Her notebook is for writing down clues.

Prince Neel is one of Mira's best friends. He's an inventor and is always coming up with new ideas, like his Flycycle.

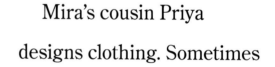

Mira's cousin Priya designs clothing. Sometimes she makes disguises that Mira wears when she's on the case.

Every time there's a mystery to solve, Mira goes on the case! She puts on her royal detective coat and badge, grabs her magnifying glass and notebook, and starts looking for clues. Mira always begins a new case by asking people questions, like . . .

"What did you see?"

"What do
you remember?"

She learns
a lot from their
answers.

Someone very wise once told Mira that a good detective must always look closer. When Mira looks closely at things, she usually finds what she's looking for.

When Mira finds a clue, she draws it in her special notebook. Then she looks at her drawings and thinks them through so she can figure out how the clues connect to each other.

Mira's father, Sahil, is the head of transportation for the royal family, which means that he is responsible for vehicles like the royal carriage. Sometimes Mira asks him to come on a case with her. Mira loves spending time with her papa!

Family is very important to Mira. She takes every opportunity she can to show her father how much she loves him—including giving him a great big hug.

Mira says goodbye to her father and runs off. She has a lot she wants to do today!

Prince Neel's older brother is named Prince Veer. He likes being in charge, and he really likes telling other people what to do.

Mira and her friends found some secret tunnels beneath the royal palace.

They love to ride a raft through the tunnels and explore.

When Mira isn't solving a case, she likes to do lots of other things, like play music with her friends. Mira plays an instrument called the tabla.

Mira and Priya love to dance. They take lessons, and sometimes they even perform onstage!

Mira's auntie Pushpa runs a boutique in Jalpur. Her daughters, Priya and Meena, help out in the shop. Meena *loves* to try on the clothing. Their baby brother, Chotu, is always giggling.

Mira's friend Kamla helps out at her mom's chai cart, where they sell tea and sweets. So does Kamla's little sister, Dimple.

Their friend Dhruv helps his mom at her flower stand. Mira has fun visiting her friends and admiring the sweets and flowers!

Mira loves to play sports with her friends. One of her favorite sports is polo, where everyone rides a horse and hits a ball with a mallet.

Poonam and Manish are two thieves who always dress in disguises. They pretend to be waiters, musicians, sculptors, and more. Luckily, they're not very good at stealing things.

Deputy Oosha is the police cow of Jalpur. Mira can call on her if she needs help with something, like taking away the thieves after they've been caught.

Everyone in Jalpur knows that if there's a mystery, Mira will be on the case, no matter what!

Bunny Bunanza

It's a beautiful day as Pip and Freddy soar through the T.O.T.S. obstacle course. They are following the one and only Super-Duper Flier, JP.

"Pip says that if we do everything you do, we might become Super-Duper Fliers, too!" Freddy calls to JP.

Suddenly, the delivery bell rings. Captain Beakman announces, "All wings on deck! We have a bunny delivery! Repeat, a bunny delivery!" Storks begin to hurry to the hangar.

"I don't get it," says Pip. "Why is everyone rushing around for one little bunny delivery?"

But this isn't one bunny delivery. "It's a bazillion bunnies!" Freddy cries gleefully. "And they're all so hippity-hoppity!" It's going to take every flier at T.O.T.S. to get all the babies to their different families.

"All right, fliers," says Captain Beakman. "Let's get these tots to their moms and pops!" The conveyor belt springs to life, carrying crates.

Pip and Freddy aren't delivering just one bunny . . .

"We're delivering one . . . two . . . three bunnies!" Freddy can't believe how cute the babies are.

They open the crates, and all three bunnies hop out. The bunnies hop all over Freddy and Pip. Freddy is excited to play with the baby bunnies!

JP, who is delivering three bunnies of his own, notices Freddy. "JP does not play with the bunnies," he says disapprovingly. "JP delivers the bunnies!"

"You heard JP," Pip tells Freddy. "If we want to be Super-Duper Fliers, we have to do exactly what he does."

"You got it," Freddy agrees. "Okay, little bunnies, into your crates!"

Pip and Freddy are
cleared for takeoff.

"Flamin-goooooo!" Freddy
calls. But the weight of the
crates flips them upside down!

With a flap of his wings, Freddy
sets them right side up again.

"Wow, look at JP! He flies
so straight," says Pip. "Let's do
exactly what he does!"

When JP notices Pip and Freddy following him, he stops in his flight path, surprised.

Uh-oh! Freddy can't slow down in time.

"We're going to crash, JP!" Pip cries.

JP, Pip, and Freddy tumble to the ground and land in a heap. Then the crates pop open and all the baby bunnies hop out! There are baby bunnies everywhere!

"The bunnies are all mixed up!" JP says. "Since we don't know whose bunnies are whose, we're going to have to deliver our bunnies . . . together."

Pip, Freddy, and JP leave one, two, three, four, five baby bunny crates on doorsteps. But when they get to the sixth house . . .

"This is not our baby," says the mama.

"There must have been a little mix-up," says JP.

The delivery birds retrace their flight path and pick up all the babies.

"We don't know which bunnies go to which families!" Freddy says. "What are we gonna do?"

"JP will know," says Pip. "Right, JP?"

"Certainly," JP says confidently. "We just need to ask them their names." JP picks up a light-colored bunny. "Is your name Burpy?" he asks. The baby looks up at him and coos. JP puts the tiny bunny in the crate labeled BURPY. Freddy, Pip, and JP continue to ask the bunnies' names until each one is sorted.

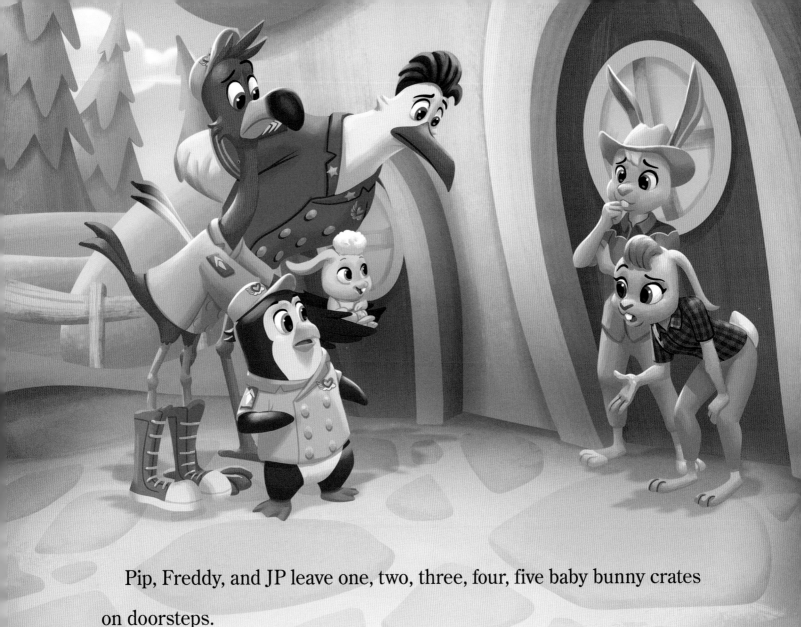

Pip, Freddy, and JP leave one, two, three, four, five baby bunny crates on doorsteps.

But when they get to the sixth house . . . "That's not our baby!" says the mama.

"Uh-oh," Freddy says. "What do we do now?"

"JP has a plan," says Pip. "Right, JP?"

JP weighs the babies. He sniffs the babies. But he can't figure out which baby bunny goes to which family!

"I have failed," JP says sadly. "Maybe I'm not super-duper after all."

Pip can't believe his ears. "Who's the fastest flier at T.O.T.S.? Who has won Delivery Bird of the Month nine times in a row? You are super-duper, JP. And we can make this delivery. But we can't do it without you."

JP smiles at Pip. "Okay, young penguin, we will give it a try."

"You are just the blinkiest bunny ever!" says Freddy to one bunny. "And you're just the bouncy-wounciest bunny of all!" he says to another.

"Freddy!" cries Pip. "I think you learned those bunnies' names by playing with them! Bouncy is bouncy, and Blinky is blinky. Maybe if we keep playing with the bunnies, we can find out who each one is!"

Pip, Freddy, and JP deliver one, two, three, four, five bunnies to their new homes. And when they get to the sixth house . . .

"Our baby!" says the mama bunny when she opens the door.

"Thank you!" says the bunny dad as he hugs his adorable little baby.

"Today you were trying to be like me," JP says to Pip and Freddy. "But I learned that perhaps I should be more like you!"

Super Adventure

Today Mickey and his pals are pretending to be superheroes.

"Superheroes work together to save the day from super villains," Mickey explains.

Donald will pretend to be the bad guy. "You'll never defeat me!" he shouts.

The superheroes chase Donald every which way.

"Wait! We're supposed to work together as a super team," Mickey says.

But the heroes don't listen and end up in a jumble. Just then, a shadow

falls over the gang.

"Gawrsh!" says Goofy. "It's a giant hot dog balloon."

"That's a zeppelin," says Mickey. "But what's it doing here?"

Suddenly, the zeppelin zaps the Glove Balloon with a shrink ray!

Power-Pants Pete flies down. "Stay back," he warns. "I'm about to shrink everything in the Clubhouse World!"

Power-Pants Pete picks up the Glove Balloon and flies off.

"We have to stop Pete from shrinking everything!" says Mickey.

Professor Von Drake has a new invention. "I have just the thingamajig you need!" he says. "I call it the Super-Maker Machine."

"It makes soup?" asks Goofy.

"No, Goofy," says the professor with a laugh. "It will make real superheroes out of all of you."

The friends step into the machine.

"Now you all have super fantastic powers!" the professor exclaims. "But you'll have to work together to stop Power-Pants Pete."

"Don't worry," says Super Mickey. "The Clubhouse Heroes are on the job!"

"One more thing," the professor adds. "You'll only have your powers for a little while. When your Superpower Bands turn red, your powers will go kaput."

"Then we'd better get going!" says Minnie.

Power-Pants Pete is about to shrink Minnie's Bow-tique! Upsy Daisy has an idea. "I'll use my mind powers to push the zeppelin."

Wonder Minnie has another idea. "My Super-Wonder Bows will stop Pete."

But neither idea works.

"You powers blocked each other," says Mickey. Suddenly, Pete drops hundreds of rubber duckies!

Mickey calls for help. Super Toodles has four Super Mouseketools—a giant blow-dryer, a catcher's mitt, a big umbrella, and a Mystery Mouseketool. "Let's try the umbrella!" says Mickey.

The big umbrella does the trick. The rubber duckies bounce right off. But Pete shrinks Minnie's Bow-tique anyway and zooms off!

The superheroes chase the zeppelin. The zeppelin lands and out comes the big boss—Megamort.

"It's shrinking time," he says. Megamort makes Pete tiny with his shrink ray.

"Oh, that tickled," says Pete.

"I'm taking the Clubhouse World for myself!" Megamort says. He jumps in the zeppelin and takes off again.

"We have to catch Megamort," says Mickey. "Our powers are almost gone!"

Megamort traps the superheroes in a superstrong bubble. Mickey needs another Mouseketool. He chooses the blow-dryer and blows the bubbles away.

Back on the ground, Tiny Pete is rolling down a hill! The heroes try to catch him, but they trip over each other.

"Tiny Pete is rolling away, and our Superpower Bands are all red!" says Daisy. In a flash, the Clubhouse Heroes lose all their superpowers!

Up in the zeppelin, Megamort takes aim at the Clubhouse. Mickey tries to stop him, but he loses his powers, too. As Mickey falls toward the ground, Megamort zaps him and the Clubhouse! Tiny Mickey tells Pluto to go find the Clubhouse Heroes. Megamort scoops up Mickey and the Clubhouse and takes them into the zeppelin.

Minnie and the rest of the friends are still trying to save Tiny Pete. But Pete hits a bump and is launched into the air! "We have to catch him!" shouts Minnie. She calls over Toodles.

Minnie chooses the catcher's mitt. She runs to catch Pete, but she's too far away. Minnie tosses the mitt to Daisy, but she's not close enough, either. Goofy grabs the mitt and makes the catch!

"We did it," says Minnie. "We worked together as a team!"

All at once, the gang is turned back into superheroes!

"When we work together," says Minnie, "we're super-duper!"

She looks up. "Uh-oh. Megamort has captured Mickey!"

"We gotta save him," says Goofy.

The gang picks the Mystery Mouseketool. It's a super jet! "Up and away," says Minnie. "Let's save the day!"

The heroes plan to work together to rescue Mickey.

Goofy and Donald sneak aboard the zeppelin and find the shrunken Clubhouse World. They quickly gather up all the globes. Megamort tries to stop them, but Tiny Mickey trips him up just in time!

The heroes bring the zeppelin to a sudden stop. Goofy, Donald, and Mickey tumble out and land right in the super jet! But the zeppelin springs a leak and flies out of control.

"Megamort needs help!" shouts Mickey.

"But he's a villain," says Goofy.

"He still needs saving," says Mickey. "And that's what heroes do!"

Pluto helps Wonder Minnie tie up the zeppelin with her Super-Wonder Bows. Then Donald and Goofy grab the ribbons and pull. Soon the rest of the gang joins them. Everyone works together and pulls the zeppelin to the ground.

"We did it!" they shout.

Megamort scrambles out of the flattened zeppelin.

"After all I did, I can't believe you rescued me," he says. "Thank you."

"You're welcome, Mr. Megamort," says Goofy.

"I'm really Mortimer Mouse," Megamort reveals. "I'm your new neighbor."

"Well, you weren't acting very neighborly," Minnie points out. Mortimer agrees. He reverses the shrink ray and returns Mickey and Pete to their normal sizes!

Then Mortimer unshrinks the whole Clubhouse World. "I'm sorry," he says. "I thought if I took what you had, I'd be happy."

"The Clubhouse is all about having friends," says Mickey.

"That's just it," Mortimer admits. "I don't have any friends."

"You do now!" says Goofy.

"That's super!" says Mortimer.

"It's more than super," says Mickey. "It's super-duper."

Vampirina

Vee's Monster Bash

"**Mama! Papa! Wake up!** Wake up!" Vampirina shouts, jumping on her parents' coffin.

Demi zooms in, too. "Yeah, wake up! Wake up!"

Vee is excited because it's the day of her costume party. They sent out invitations to all their Transylvanian friends weeks ago. Vee reminds them that her human friends Poppy and Bridget are coming to the party, too.

"Well then, I guess it's a good thing Mama and I stayed up all night decorating," says Boris with a smile.

When Vee gets downstairs, she's amazed! Spooky fog fills the living room, creepy spiders float through the air, cauldrons bubble over with green potion, and enchanted brooms dance around the house.

"It's spooktacular!" Vee exclaims. "I can't wait for my friends to see it! This is going to be the best party ever!"

Suddenly, Vee stops and says to Demi, "Now that we live in Pennsylvania, what if our human neighbors spot our Transylvanian monster friends and get spooked?"

"Don't worry," Demi says. "The humans will probably think the monsters are just humans dressed up as monsters for your costume party!"

Vee hopes Demi is right.

Eeeeek!

The Hauntleys' doorbell screams. Their first guests have arrived! Vee opens the door.

"AHHH!" Demi shrieks. "Cowgirl! Giant cat!"

Vee explains that it's just Poppy and Bridget in their costumes.

"Where's your costume, Vee?" Poppy asks.

Vee shrugs. "We're kind of in ours year-round," she says, "being vampires and all."

Vee's doorbell shrieks again. "Our monster guests must be here!" she says.

Soon the Hauntleys' house is full of ghouls. There are mummies, goblins, witches, and even Vee's favorite band from Transylvania, the Scream Girls!

"You came all the way here for my party?" Vee squeals.

"We wouldn't miss it!" Franken-Stacey says.

The doorbell shrieks again. Vee opens the door, expecting more monster guests. But instead she finds the Hauntleys' neighbors Edna, Edgar, and Ms. Meyer.

"We heard about your little costume party and thought it would be fun to drop in," says Edna.

Vee panics. The entire house is full of spooky enchanted decorations! "I think having a monster party in Pennsylvania was a bad idea," she tells her parents. "We have to hide everything!"

Boris hides the hovering headstones. Oxana covers the bubbling cauldrons.

And Vee corners the conga-dancing broomsticks.

Just then, Vee sees Edna and Ms. Meyer

mingling with the monster guests. Edgar is even dancing with a little

witch. "Cool costume," he says to the witch.

"They must think all the monsters are just humans wearing costumes,"

Vee says to her mom and dad, relieved.

Humans and monsters boogie together like old friends.

But then Vee spots her pet werewolf, Wolfie!

"Oh, no! Wolfie's going to scare Edgar!" she says.

Before she can stop him, Wolfie bounds over to Edgar and gives him a big slobbery lick. Instead of screaming, Edgar smiles. "Someone else came as a werewolf? Cool! We can be a pack!" he declares.

Then Edgar and Wolfie actually howl together.

Eeeeek!

It's Vampirina's doorbell again. This time, it's Dr. Paquette, the
critternarian from Transylvania. Vee is relieved it's not another human.

"I hope you don't mind, but I brought Brocknar, too!" says Dr. P.

"Brocknar?" Vampirina asks, craning her neck to look up at Brocknar,
who happens to be an enormous dragon.

"Oh, no! There's no way any of the humans will think that is a costume!"

Vee says, worried. "We can't let everybody see a real fire-breathing dragon!"

Vee and her friends have to hide Brocknar . . . but where?

When guests walk outside, Poppy is sitting on Brocknar's back.

"Who's up for a ride on my remote-control dragon?" shouts Vee, hoping no one will be scared away.

They try to stuff Brocknar in the attic, but he's too squished.

They put Brocknar in Vee's bedroom, but the dust makes him sneeze.

Just then, Vee has an idea. They sneak Brocknar out to the backyard.

The humans have no idea Brocknar is real, and everybody loves him!

"You sure know how to throw a great monster bash!" says Poppy.

"Thanks!" says Vee. "Humans and monsters may be different, but everyone likes to have fun!"

Head Nurse Hallie

It's a busy day at the Toy Hospital. Doc is about to make notes on Tony the Taxi's chart when she notices something. "Oh, no! I grabbed the wrong chart!"

Good thing Nurse Hallie has the right chart ready. "Here's the one you need."

"Oh, Hallie, what would I do without you?"

Hallie winks. "Well, lucky for you, you're never gonna have to find out. You're my Doc, and I'm your Hallie!"

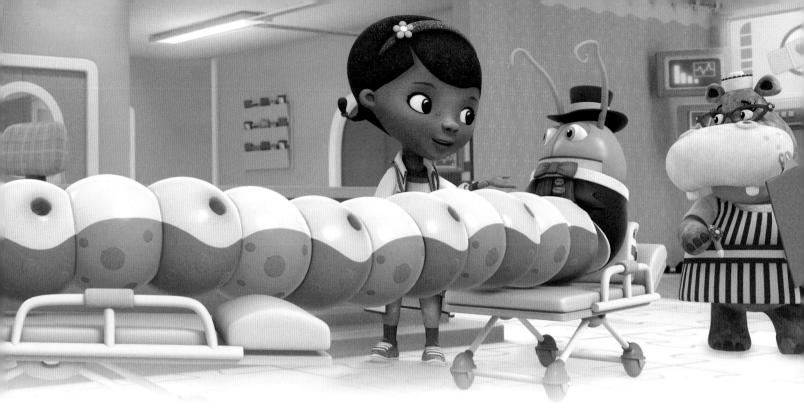

Just then, Doc's toy-sponder beeps and sparkles. That means a patient is coming in and needs help. Hallie follows Doc down the hall.

Rosie the ambulance and Darla, the emergency medical toy technician, arrive with the new patient.

Doc and Hallie rush their very long patient into the exam room. Then Hallie begins to fill out a chart. "Male. Plastic. Vitals are stable."

Doc examines the toy. "Our patient appears to be a wiggly worm toy, but something's wrong. . . ."

Suddenly, Darla hands Hallie a jumble of colorful legs. The patient isn't a worm—he is a caterpillar!

The caterpillar nods. "Leggy Leo's what they call me. But I'm not so leggy without my legs!"

Doc examines a leg. "This looks like a case of Leggy-Pops!"

Leo squirms on the table. "Without legs, I don't have shoes! And without my shoes, I can't do my famous caterpillar tap dance!"

"Don't worry, Leo. I'll make sure you can tap-dance again."

Using her toy-sponder, Doc
calls for extra help.

Before long, Stuffy, Lambie,
and Chilly show up and join
Doc and Hallie in the exam
room. Doc smiles at her toys.
"Everybody ready?"

"I am!"

Everyone turns around to see
who else has come to help. It is
an adorable plush rhino dressed
in nurse's scrubs. She introduces
herself. "I'm Riley Rhino,
registered rhino nurse. I came to
lend a helping hand!"

Hallie starts to give out orders. "We've got the Leggy-Pops, people! Stuffy, you're in charge of Leo's chart. Lambie, you're on standby for cuddles. And, Leo, you just relax, sugar."

Doc looks at her patient. "Okay, Leo, I'm going to snap your leg back on. Everybody, watch and learn how I do it."

Stuffy leans over the table to get a better look. "Watching and learning—whoaaaa!"

Stuffy watches as Doc puts
one of Leo's legs back in place.
Then Stuffy snaps one of Leo's
legs back on.

"Nice kicks you got here, Leo.
Better check your reflexes."

Stuffy taps on the leg with a hammer. And off pops the leg! Stuffy panics.
"Duh-oh! Leg on the loose!"

The leg soars toward Hallie. But
before she can catch it, Nurse
Riley intercepts it!

Hallie shakes her head. "I'm
always one step ahead of Doc,
but now Riley's one step
ahead of me!"

Next Doc tells her helpers that Leo's legs need to be in the right order,
like the colors of a rainbow.

Hallie jumps up and grabs
a rolling tray. "I'm on a
roll with it, Doc!"

But Riley cuts her off. "Already done, Hallie. Red, yellow, green, and blue! Right as a rainbow!"

Doc is pleased. "Oh, wow! That's great, Nurse Riley."

Riley smiles. "I'm here to help, Doc!"

As Hallie rolls her tray away, she feels sad. "But if Riley's here to help Doc, then Doc won't need me anymore."

Meanwhile, Doc reaches for the next of Leo's legs. "Uh-oh. This one's cracked. Leo, you have a slight case of Cracked-Leg-Peg-osis."

Hallie knows just what to do next. She rushes over to get the Big Book of Boo-Boos. But Riley beats her to it! "Here's a fresh page for you, Doc!"

As Doc draws in the book, Hallie hangs her head. "I guess Doc doesn't need much of me anymore." Then, without anyone noticing, she leaves.

Doc wraps tape around Leo's cracked leg and then snaps the rest of his legs back on. "Leo, your legs are secure!"

Leo wiggles his feet happily. "Aw, thanks, Doc! And thanks, Nurse Riley!"

Riley blushes. "Oh, thank you. I still have a whole lot to learn."

Doc pipes up. "You can learn from the best nurse I know: Hallie!"

Riley agrees. "It would be a pleasure to learn from Nurse Hallie. Everybody knows she's the best nurse around!"

But when Doc turns to talk to Hallie, she doesn't see her hippo helper anywhere. "That's strange. Hmmm. Where did she go?"

Stuffy looks around the room. Lambie is concerned. Doc is, too. "We need to find her."

Nurse Riley offers to stay behind with Leo and get him to the recovery room.

Doc turns to the other toys. "Okay, guys. Let's go!" Doc and the toys leave the hospital to look around the town square.

The toys walk into the Plush Beauty Salon. To everyone's surprise, Hallie is working there.

Doc walks over to her. "Hallie, what are you doing here?"

Hallie shrugs. "Just thought I'd try something new."

"But, Hallie, you're not a hairdresser. You're a nurse!"

Hallie puts her brush down. "I thought I'd be the only nurse you'd ever need. But now you've got Riley. I figured you didn't need me anymore."

"Of course I need you! I'll always need you!" Doc said. "We're running a big hospital now, and I need more than one nurse. But I need my best hippo nurse more than ever. So will you come back to the hospital?"

Before Hallie can answer, Doc's toy-sponder beeps and sparkles. Nurse Riley is hurt back at the hospital.

"Hallie, are you with us?"

"I don't know, Doc. I have a customer. . . ."

Back at the hospital, Doc finds Riley with a twisted, squished rhino horn.

"Nurse Riley, what happened?"

Riley explains. "I was wheeling Leo to recovery when I slipped, tripped, and took a tumble."

Doc examines Riley's horn. "It looks like you've twisted your horn pretty badly. But don't worry, Riley. You'll be fine. I just need to get a closer look with my—"

"Magnifying glass, Doc?"

"Hallie! You came back!"

Hallie beams. "Doc and Hallie. Hallie and Doc.'"

Then it's time to fix Riley's horn. "There aren't any rips in your stitching, but you do have a case of Rhino-Twisty."

Nurse Hallie springs into action. "Let's untwist that diagnosis in the Big Book of Boo-Boos!"

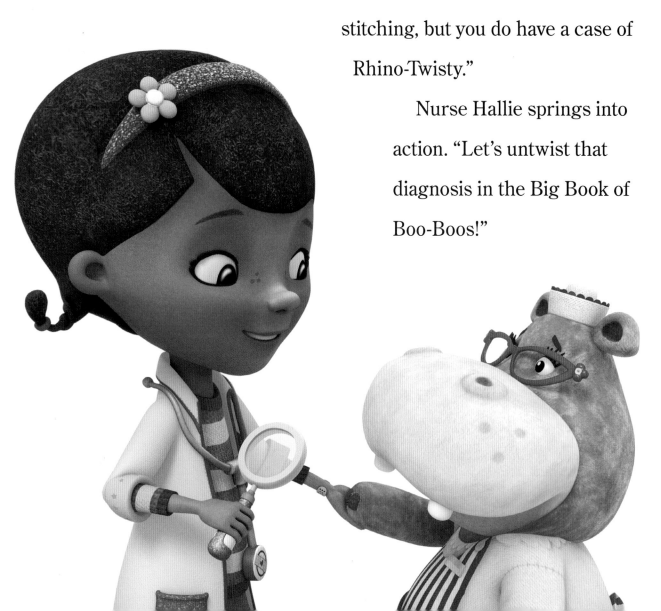

The other toys watch as Doc untwists Riley's horn. Riley touches her horn with amazement. "Thanks, Doc McStuffins! A happy horn is a happy rhino!"

Doc shrugs. "I couldn't have done it without Hallie."

Riley turns to Hallie. "Gee, I hope I'm a nurse like you someday. Everyone knows you're the best. Just look at the way you take charge and lead your team!"

That gives Doc McStuffins a great idea. "Hallie, I'd like to promote you to be head nurse of the McStuffins Toy Hospital."

"Oh!" Hallie blushes with pride. "Doc, this is a huge hippo honor! Being a nurse is what I do best—and being head nurse is what I'll do better!"

Everyone cheers. "Head Nurse Hallie!"

Song of the Sirenas

Elena arrives in Nueva Vista to visit her cousin Cristóbal.
Elena gives her cousin a big hug. "I've missed you, *Primo*."

"And I've missed all of you," he says. "Which is why we are
throwing a big parade tomorrow
to honor you for defeating
Shuriki."

Elena tells him that
Shuriki is not as defeated
as they thought: the
wicked sorceress is still
out there somewhere.

"But you have a
secret weapon,"
Cristóbal
says. "It's your
familia."

Meanwhile, Elena's jaquin friends, Migs, Skylar, and Luna, fly toward Nueva Vista. "Remember, this isn't a vacation," Migs reminds them. "We have to protect our princess in case of—"

"Shuriki!" yells Skylar. He sees the wicked sorceress directly below them with her friends Victor and Carla Delgado and the dark wizard Fiero.

Shuriki points her scepter at the jaquins. "Obscure!" she shouts. A red mist surrounds them, and when it clears, Shuriki and her friends are gone.

"We better tell the princess," says Luna.

Elena can't believe what her friends are telling her. "Shuriki's *here*?" she gasps. "Maybe we should cancel the parade." But Cristóbal refuses. The people have waited too long to see their princess. He promises to increase security.

After talking to Cristóbal, Elena is walking along the main canal when she hears mysterious singing. Elena follows the voices to find two Sirenas waiting for her. "What's happening?" she says.

"Please don't be scared," one of the Sirenas tells Elena. "I'm Princess Marisa, and this is my brother, Prince Marzel."

"I'm sure you've heard of all the terrible things Sirenas have done," Marisa says. "But that's not the whole story."

She explains that their mother was human and their father is king of the Sirenas. "Our mom convinced the

Sirenas to stop sinking human ships," Marisa continues. "We were hoping you could tell them that we've changed. It's time to have peace between humans and Sirenas."

Elena promises to bring her cousin to meet them and hear their story.

Cristóbal agrees to meet the Sirenas, but moments after he and Elena arrive at the cove, he calls his guards. "Seize them!" Marzel and Marisa escape.

Elena turns to Cristóbal, furious. "Why did you do that? The Sirenas came to discuss peace."

"I've been dealing with Sirenas my whole life. They cannot be trusted. I did it to protect you," Cristóbal insists.

Elena trusts her cousin and is wary of the Sirenas.

The next morning is the day of the masquerade parade. As the guest of honor, Elena will ride in the very last float.

But as the floats begin the parade into the city, Elena and her friends are shocked to see Shuriki everywhere! Dozens of people are dressed up as her for the parade.

"How will we spot the real Shuriki?" Elena asks.

"I see some of her no-good friends!" Gabe shouts. He goes after them with Naomi, Mateo, and the jaquins.

Elena is all alone when she sees two figures emerge from the shadows. It's Shuriki and Fiero. They begin to battle. Elena can't fight two sorcerers at once. She points her scepter at herself. "Vanish!" Elena disappears . . . almost.

Shuriki spots Elena's tiara midair and smiles. She and Fiero cast spells on Elena at the same time! Elena is knocked unconscious and falls off her float into the water.

Suddenly, two arms reach out and pull Elena from the depths. It's Marisa! She takes Elena to a field of magical kelp.

Marisa starts wrapping kelp around Elena's chest so she can breathe.

A few moments later, Elena opens her eyes and looks around. "Where am I?"

she asks, dazed. "Shuriki is back. I need to stop her!"

Marisa wants to help prove the Sirenas have changed. She takes Elena to the surface. "This is my chance to show humans we want peace. I've got to take it."

"Then let's go," Elena says.

Marisa and Elena find Cristóbal, who has the Scepter of Light.

"Shuriki is here," Elena says. "But don't worry. I'll stop her!"

But Cristóbal throws the scepter into the ocean. "When Shuriki ruled Avalor, she gave

me gold in return for my loyalty," Cristóbal tells her. "When you got rid of her, you also got rid of my gold supply." Then he signals for his guards to grab her.

Marisa tries to help. "The wicked Sirena is trying to attack our princess!" Cristóbal shouts.

"Take Elena to the palace and lock up that Sirena!" No one notices Marzel watching from the water.

Cristóbal throws Elena and Marisa in the tower cell, where the rest of Elena's family has already been imprisoned.

Soon after Cristóbal leaves, a magical blast blows a hole in the ceiling. Mateo holds up his *tamborita*. He uses a lifting spell to float everyone out of the tower cell.

By the time Cristóbal brings Shuriki to the cell, it's empty.

97

Elena and her friends and
family return to their ship.
"Sail back to Avalor City as
fast as you can!" Elena says.

But it doesn't take long for Shuriki to find them, and Elena does not have her scepter. Shuriki looms closer and closer, and there is nothing the princess can do about it.

Shuriki grins, tasting victory. "Infer—"

The ship lurches to the side, and Shuriki cries out. The song of the Sirenas has caused the ship to go off course. Shuriki falls, and her blast misses Elena.

The Sirenas continue to sing, and the captain falls under their spell and turns the ship toward the shore.

"No!" cries Cristóbal. "My yacht! My palace!" Everyone abandons ship.

"Follow them!" calls Gabe.

"Elena, catch!" calls Marzel, tossing her the scepter. With the Scepter of Light in hand, Elena is ready for Shuriki— again.

Elena faces off against Shuriki. "We must stop meeting like this, Elena," Shuriki growls.

"Don't worry. We will," Elena says confidently. "Blaze!"

"Goodbye, Elena. Demolish!"

At that exact moment, Elena whispers, "Vanish."

Shuriki looks all around, but there is no sign of Elena. Until . . .

"Missed me. Blast!" Elena lands a direct hit on Shuriki. The evil sorceress is finally defeated for good.

Guards arrest Cristóbal. "Let me go!" he demands. "I'm familia!"

"You have no idea what that word means," Elena tells him. Then she turns to the Sirenas. "Let this be remembered as the day Sirenas and humans defended Avalor together and began a new era of friendship!"

"I look forward to a new era of peace, on land and sea," the king of the Sirenas says.

"I've dreamt of this day for so long," Marisa says.

Elena nods and tells her, "Sometimes dreams come true."

Elena breathes a sigh of relief that she had defeated Shuriki. Avalor is safe at last!

The Last Pup-icorn

Keia is the new puppy in town. She just moved in next door to Bingo and Rolly. Keia loves her owner Chloe more than anything in the world!

Chloe has something special for Keia: a tiny unicorn costume.

"There, now you're my pup-icorn!" Chloe says. "My mom got me this because she knows how much I wish I had a unicorn."

Keia wags her tail. "I wish you had a unicorn, too!"

Chloe waves goodbye and leaves for school.

"I wish I could do something special for Chloe like you do for Bob," says Keia.

"Keia, I've got an idea!" Bingo says. "We can go on a mission!"

"That sounds amazing!" Keia replies. "If Chloe wants a unicorn, then I'm going on a mission to get her one."

MISSION: FIND A UNICORN FOR CHLOE

"We're going on a mission!" the puppies sing.

There's just one problem. . . .

"Where do we find a unicorn?" Keia wonders.

Bingo and Rolly know that A.R.F. always knows.

"A.R.F. does not know where to find a unicorn," A.R.F. tells them. "But A.R.F. does know that the unicorn of the sea lives deep in the cold, cold Arctic Ocean."

"Find the sea unicorn in the Arctic Ocean," Rolly says. "How hard can that be?"

The three puppies board a ship and keep lookout from the deck. When Rolly sees a horn pop out of the water, he shouts, "Sea unicorn, over there!" They activate their scuba gear.

One by one, the puppies dive in to the ocean. Keia is so excited to meet the sea unicorn.

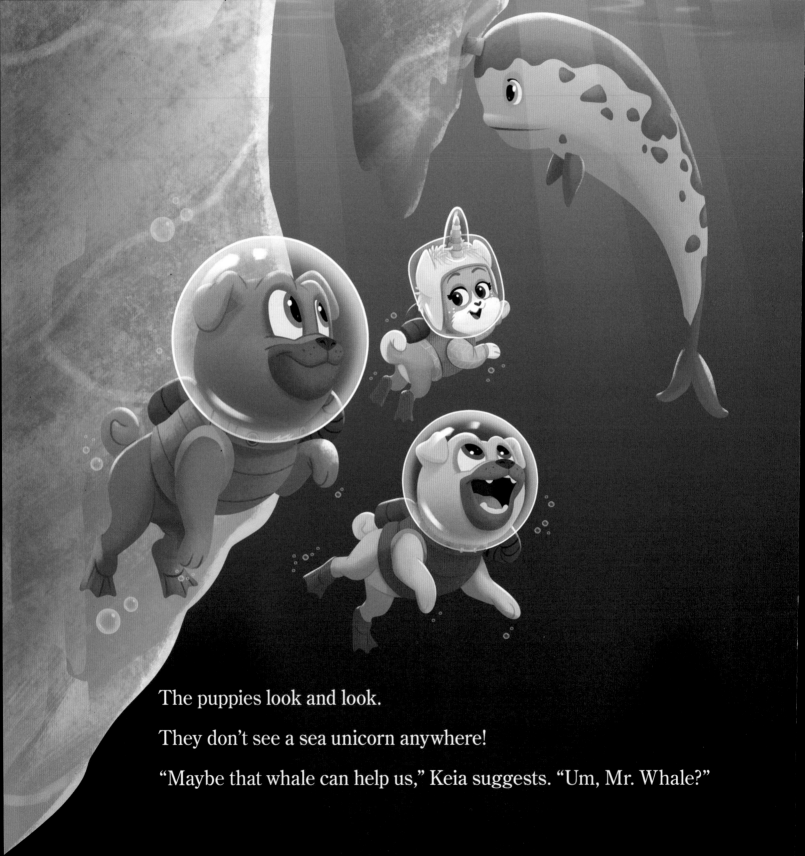

The puppies look and look.

They don't see a sea unicorn anywhere!

"Maybe that whale can help us," Keia suggests. "Um, Mr. Whale?"

When the whale turns around, Keia gasps as she sees his giant horn. "You're the sea unicorn!" she squeals.

"Actually, I'm a narwhal," the whale explains. "I'm just called the unicorn of the sea because of my horn. Fun fact: it's really a tooth!"

"I bet he uses a lot of toothpaste," Rolly whispers to his brother.

"Come to think of it, the unicorn on Chloe's sweater did look a lot more like a horse than a whale," Keia admits.

"Perhaps a horse might know more about unicorns than I do," the narwhal says.

Bingo and Rolly know some horses. Maybe they know where to find a unicorn!

"Thank you, Mr. Sea Unicorn!" Keia calls. "I mean, Mr. Narwhal!"

"Don't forget to floss!" Rolly adds.

Bingo, Rolly, and Keia head back home and run straight to the park.

"Horses!" Keia yells.

Bingo and Rolly greet their friend Betty. "Do you know where to find a unicorn?" Rolly asks her.

"There's one right next to you," she replies.

"I'm a puppy dressed like a unicorn," Keia explains.

"What will they think of next?" Betty neighs.

Betty has never seen a unicorn. But her friend Bea points to the other side of the park, where the Medieval Faire is going on.

Keia gasps in awe when she sees a magical creature in the distance. Then she takes off running.

"I'm so excited!" Keia says.

Bingo and Rolly thank Betty and Bea for their help.

Bingo and Rolly race after Keia through the Medieval Faire. It's hard not to get distracted by balls to fetch and delicious-looking turkey legs.

"Mr. Unicorn, Mr. Unicorn!" Keia calls.

"You may call me Reginald, m'lady," the unicorn replies.

"Would you come to my house to be Chloe's unicorn, please?" Keia asks him. "She loves, loves, LOVES unicorns!"

Reginald tells Keia that he would be honored to meet Chloe. "Hop aboard," he says. "Tallyho, puppy pals!"

Reginald rears. He shakes his flowing mane. And then . . .

Reginald's horn and mane fall to the ground!

"You're not a unicorn, either?" Keia asks sadly.

"Alas, I am merely a humble horse pretending to be a unicorn,"
Reginald explains. "I don't think anyone's ever seen a real unicorn."

Keia walks away, heartbroken. If no one has ever seen a unicorn, she will never find one for Chloe.

"You know, Keia," Bingo says, "with or without a unicorn, you'll always be perfect for Chloe. She's your person, and you're her puppy."

"You do give Chloe the best puppy licks," Rolly points out.

"And you make the best things out of sticks," Bingo adds.

"Sticks!" Keia shouts.

"That's it!"

Chloe runs to the craft table at the fair. She grabs a few short sticks, a few long ones, and one pointy, horn-shaped stick. Then she gets to work.

"Now Chloe can have her unicorn!" Keia says.

"Pup-tastic!" Rolly cheers.

When Chloe gets home from school, she sees the unicorn Keia made for her. She loves it! But not nearly as much as she loves her puppy.

MISSION ACCOMPLISHED.

A Walk in the Park

Minnie is dog-sitting Ella and her two furry friends. Everyone is helping in the Bow-tique—except the dogs.

"Yikes!" says Daisy. "Now we'll never get our work done!"

"Not to worry," Minnie tells everyone. "They just need a little fresh air and sunshine. Let's go for a walk in the park."

"Minnie, this was a great idea!" says Daisy as the group strolls along a lovely path.

"And the dogs look so happy!" Millie says.

They're all enjoying the beautiful day when, suddenly, Cuckoo-Loca cries out, "Hot dog!"

"Well, they feel okay to me," Daisy says as she feels each of the pooches' foreheads.

"Not these dogs,"
Cuckoo-Loca says. "Those!"
She points to a cart full of
delicious steaming hot dogs.
Minnie smiled.

"Oh!" says Daisy. "Well,
I am getting hungry."

"Me too," adds
Minnie.

"Me three," says Millie.

"Me four," Melody says.
"I love hot dogs!"

The group heads over to the hot-dog
cart. Minnie counts up everyone and turns to the vendor. "Five hot dogs,
please," she says.

"Comin' right up," the hot-dog man replies.

Minnie and her friends are not the only ones who are hungry. As each hot dog is prepared, Ella inches closer and closer to the food cart.

The hot dogs are just too yummy to pass up! Ella springs into the air, nabbing one from the cart.

"Hey!" the hot-dog man yells. "Where do you think you're going with that?"

Ella breaks free from Minnie and runs off. Carrying the hot dog in her mouth, Ella sprints through the park, away from Minnie and the rest of the group.

When the other dogs get a whiff of Ella's hot dog, they chase her through the park.

"Runaway dogs!" Cuckoo-Loca cries.

"We've got to catch them!" Minnie says.

"And fast!" Cuckoo-Loca adds. Minnie, Daisy, and the twins run after the dogs.

The dogs have a pretty big head start. Minnie worries they might not able to catch them.

The dogs zip and zoom around the park so quickly that no one can keep up.

"They're headed thataway!" Cuckoo-Loca calls.

"To the tennis court!" Melody adds.

Ella leaps across the tennis court and lands on the switch of the tennis ball launcher!

The machine rumbles and whirs. Then . . .

. . . tennis balls bounce everywhere! The dogs are thrilled.

"Watch out, Millie!" Melody calls.

"You too!" Millie replies.

Finally, Minnie makes her way to the launcher and shuts it off.

"What a mess!" she exclaims.

"Thank goodness things are finally under control," Daisy says.

Just then, a squirrel with a big twitchy tail catches Ella's eye. Ella begins tugging and pulling at her leash. Daisy clutches the leashes and digs her heels into the ground, but it's no use. . . .

A new chase is on! The dogs tear after the squirrel, pulling Daisy behind them.

"Whoa! This walk in the park is no walk in the park!" cries Daisy.

The dogs run Daisy in circles around the fountain, trees, bushes, and flowers. They race through a picnic. Food flies everywhere! But the dogs don't even notice.

The squirrel runs through the park playground, and the dogs chase after it, dragging poor Daisy along until a ride on the spinning carousel sends her flying!

Daisy lands with a thud in the sandbox. She forgets where she is!

"Welcome to my castle," she says.

"Let's go for a park in the walk."

"Are you okay, Daisy?" Minnie asks.

"Just fine . . . I think," Daisy replies.

"This is not goody-good at all," Daisy says as her friends dust her off.

"Those dogs might chase that squirrel forever!" says Millie.

"And I can't fly much longer," Cuckoo-Loca says. "It's too hot to keep chasing these dogs."

"Hot . . . dogs," Minnie says, deep in thought. "That's it! Hot dogs! I know exactly how to round up Ella and the other dogs. I'll need everyone's help."

"Ready, everyone?" Minnie asks.

"Ready," says Daisy.

"Me too," says Cuckoo-Loca.

"Me three," says Millie.

"Me four," adds Melody.

"Okay. It's snack time!" Minnie announces.

Daisy and the twins take armfuls of hot dogs to the tennis ball machine.

When the launcher is loaded and ready . . . *ka-blam!*

Minnie shoots the hot dogs into the air. One by one, they sail through the sky. The dogs leap up to catch the delicious treats.

"That was a great

idea, Aunt Minnie!" says Melody.

"Now we can finish our walk," Minnie sighs.

"Because there's nothing dogs love more than a nice, relaxing walk,"

Daisy says.

"Except chasing a cat!" cries Millie, who notices Ella is staring at a kitty.

"Uh-oh," says Melody.

"Triple uh-oh," Cuckoo-Loca says.

"Not again!" cries Daisy.

"Well, everyone," Minnie says, "I guess we'll have to finish our work tomorrow. This day has gone to the dogs!"

Undercover Princess

Mira is a little girl with a big job: royal detective! She helps people around her city, Jalpur, by solving mysteries. One sunny morning, Mira gets called to the palace by Queen Shanti. The queen must have a new case for her! Mira's mongoose friends, Mikku and Chikku, come along.

The queen asks Mira to come to the royal party and stay on the lookout for anyone who tries to steal the Gem of Jalpur. "But I think you should blend in with the guests," says the queen. "I would like you to go undercover . . . as a princess!"

Mira is surprised. She's not sure how to act like a princess. Queen Shanti tells her not to worry. Prince Neel will give her royal training. Mira is ready to get started right away!

Prince Neel and his older brother, Prince Veer, meet Mira at her house. Mira has to stand up straight, wear a lot of heavy jewelry, and walk and talk like a princess. It is hard work!

After a lot of practice, Neel and Veer think Mira is finally ready. Mira gets a new princess dress and a secret identity. "It is my pleasure to introduce . . . Princess Heera!" Neel announces.

Mira isn't the only one going undercover. Her cousin Priya is assisting Princess Heera in a lady-in-waiting disguise. And Mikku and Chikku are dressed as royal food servers!

"We're happy to help," says Mikku, "especially if we get to be near the snacks!"

Mira arrives at the royal party in disguise. Kings, queens, princes, and princesses watch her enter the palace. No one has ever seen this princess before!

"Hello, Princess Heera," Queen Shanti says with a wink. Then she whispers, "Good luck finding the thieves, Mira!"

Mira goes to check on the Gem of Jalpur. "The gem is exactly where it should be," she says.

"So far, so good!" says Priya.

"Hey, I found the thief!" says Mikku. "It's Chikku! He just stole one of my snacks."

Mira laughs and reminds them to be on the lookout for anyone trying to steal the gem—not the food.

Mira and Priya separate from Mikku and Chikku and go back to the party. They have a job to do.

A group of musicians begins to play onstage. Then they walk among the party guests with their instruments. The music is lovely, and everyone is enjoying it. Suddenly, a musician trips and falls over. "Oops!" she says. "I'm so clumsy!" Everyone turns to look as a royal guard rushes

over and helps her up. The musician gets back up and brushes herself off. She is okay.

In the commotion, Mira realizes no one is guarding the Gem of Jalpur.

Mira and her friends rush back to the glass case. They are relieved to find the gem inside. But Mira notices something strange. "Isn't the Gem of Jalpur blue?" Neel nods—it is.

"Then we have a big problem," says Mira, "because this gem is green!" Mira goes to tell the queen that the Gem of Jalpur has been replaced with a fake. Queen Shanti tells Mira that she believes in her and knows she will find the real gem.

Mira and her friends check the crime scene for clues. Mira finds a red tassel on the floor.

Maybe whoever stole the gem has red tassels on their clothing. Mira tells her friends to spread out and look for more.

Mikku and Chikku find a tassel on a tray of desserts they served to the musicians.

Mira uses her magnifying glass to find another one on the stage.

"It looks like the same person who was near the gem also took dessert from Chikku and was on the stage."

"Let's think this through!" Mira says. "We found red tassels in three places: by the gem case, on the food tray, and on the stage. And there's only one person who was in all three of these places: the musician who was playing in the crowd. And his instrument has red tassels on it! We need to talk to him."

Mira finds the musicians, but they run
out the palace door before she
can ask them anything.

Mira calls for backup. "Deputy Oosha, stop them!" she cries.

The police cow comes and steps out in front of the musicians, blocking their path. "Moooooo!" Deputy Oosha cried loudly.

Startled, the two musicians stumble backward and then fall to the ground. They can't escape now!

Mira and her friends run up to the musicians. "Excuse me," Mira says, "did you steal the Gem of Jalpur?"

"Of course not!" says the drummer. "Besides, if I did steal it, where is it now?"

Mira points to the blue gem in his turban. "Right there. Your friend pretended to trip so everyone would be distracted. Then, when no one was looking, you replaced the blue Gem of Jalpur with the fake green one."

Case closed.

Mira hands the gem to Queen Shanti.

"Brilliant job, Mira," says the queen. "I knew you would solve this case.

Deputy Oosha, take them away."

"Mooo!" says Deputy Oosha.

Now that the gem has been returned to Queen Shanti, she puts it on and shows it to her guests. "Ladies and gentlemen, I'm happy to present the Royal Gem of Jalpur!"

Everyone at the party is amazed by the beautiful precious stone.

Queen Shanti asks Mira to come up onstage with her. "Earlier tonight, two thieves tried to steal the gem," the queen says. "But they didn't get away with it, thank to our royal detective, Mira!"

Everyone in the crowd gasps. They had no idea that Princess Heera was really the royal detective of Jalpur.

Hooray for Mira! She solved the case again.

Hawaii Pug-O

"**Surf's up, Rolly!**" **says** Bingo, racing through the house on his doggy skateboard.

"Bow to the wow, Bingo! I'm right on your tail!" Rolly calls.

Suddenly, their boards catch on the rug, sending them sailing through the air . . . and into their owner's bed.

"I'm awake! I'm awake!" Bob says, sitting up. "Now there are two little fellas I like seeing early in the morning."

At breakfast, Bob sees a newspaper ad about Hawaii. "Big waves, sandy beaches," he says dreamily. "I sure would love to feel the sand between my toes." But Bob can't go to Hawaii today. He has to go to work.

As soon as Bob leaves, Bingo turns to Rolly. "We have a mission! We need to go to Hawaii to get sand for Bob's toes!"

"'Cause happy toes means happy Bob!" says Rolly.

MISSION: GET HAWAIIAN SAND FOR BOB'S TOES

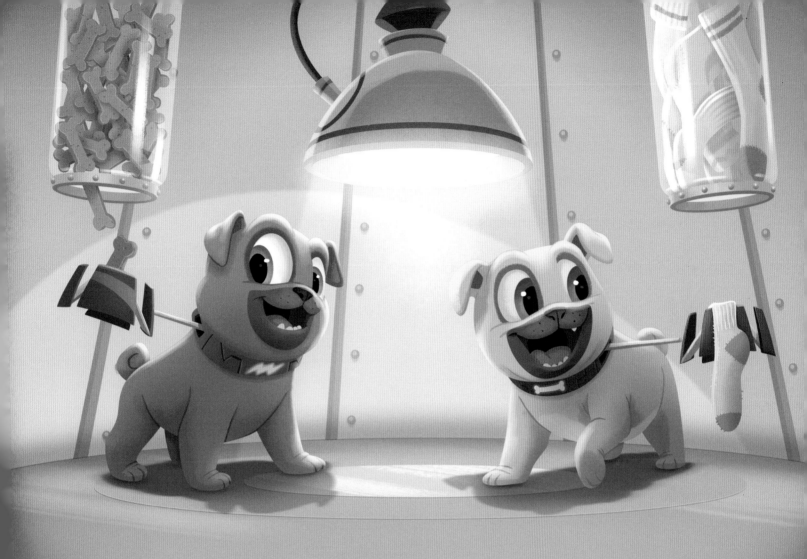

They run to the doghouse to get ready for their mission. One of Bob's inventions puts special collars on the pugs and then fills compartments in the collars with dog treats.

Rolly tosses an old sock into another compartment. "I always feel better carrying an old sock," he says.

"Who doesn't?" Bingo agrees. They are ready to roll.

The pups race to the airport. They've got to find a plane to Hawaii. A couple walks by with suitcases. "We're going to Hawaii!" the woman says.

Bingo and Rolly leap into the woman's bag.

When the plane lands, the pugs run down the steps, excited for the next part of their mission!

A hop, skip, and jump later, Bingo and Rolly arrive at the beach.

"Look at all this sand!" says Bingo. "It's perfect for Bob's toes!"

But Rolly is not thinking about Bob. He's thinking about catching a sand crab.

Bingo is focused on the mission at hand. "Now we just have to get this sand home," he says. "We need something big that flies. Let's get to work."

Bingo and Rolly decide to make their own airplane—out of sand!

"Now we can fly all this sand back to Bob!" Rolly exclaims.

"Let's go!" says Bingo.

Rolly's eyes get wide. "Wave!"

"Right! Let's wave goodbye to everyone," Bingo agrees.

"No!" Rolly says, pointing to the ocean. "Wave!"

With their airplane gone, the puppies decide they need a boat instead. They build one out of sand. But before they can set sail, another wave crashes over them!

"We came to get sand for Bob, so why are you walking away?" Bingo asks.

"I'm not. You are!" Rolly replies.

But neither of the puppies is walking anywhere. . . .

They're floating away!

The puppies wonder how they are going to get sand for Bob when they are so far away from the shore. They begin to paddle as best they can.

Just then, a dog on a surfboard floats by. "Aloha, puppy dudes! You here for the surfing contest?" he asks.

"We've never surfed for real before," Rolly says.

"It's just like riding our skateboards!" says Bingo confidently. "Hang pup!" The puppies brace themselves. This is going to be fun!

Bingo and Rolly ride a wave to shore, howling for joy the whole way.

When they reach the beach, a trophy is waiting for them. They won the surfing contest!

Rolly shrugs. "We must've gotten bonus points for being extra huggable."

"This trophy's cool," says Bingo, "but we still need to bring back sand for Bob's toes."

Rolly is still on a mission to catch the crab. Rolly starts to dig, sending sand flying through the air—and into the trophy.

"Hey, this is the perfect way to get the sand back to Bob," Bingo says. "Keep digging!"

"Anything for you, brother!" Rolly says, digging faster and faster until the trophy is full.

The pups take the trophy full of sand back home.

Their mission is complete! They're about to go into the house when the

gardener walks by with a leaf blower. He accidentally blows all the sand away!

"It's gone. All of it," Bingo says sadly.

"Except for the sand that's still in my ears," says Rolly.

"Yeah," Bingo agrees. "We really got covered in that stuff!" The puppies scratch and shake, sending the sand flying. Suddenly, Bingo gets an idea!

The puppies run inside to wait for Bob to come home from work.

"Hey, guys!" Bob says happily as he walks in the door. "I've been looking forward to seeing you all day."

Bingo and Rolly look at each other, nod, and then shake, shake, shake! Bob starts laughing. "How in the world did you two get so sandy?"

"Now there's sand everywhere—even between my toes!" says Bob. "But you know, that feels pretty good." He wiggles his toes and smiles. "Must be how the beach in Hawaii would feel."

Bingo and Rolly look at each other and smile.

MISSION ACCOMPLISHED.

Realm of the Jaquins

Elena is at Mooncliff to watch the jaquins' guardian test. Skylar's younger brother, Nico, is taking the test to become a guardian of Avalor. He passes his first test with flying colors.

But during the next test, disaster strikes. Victor and Carla Delgado, longtime enemies of Avalor, hide in the jungle and ruin Nico's test.

Elena thinks Nico deserves a second chance, but Migs and Luna shake their heads. King Verago, the leader of the jaquins, does not allow second chances.

"I'll just ask King Verago to make an exception!"

The jaquins warn Elena that humans are not allowed in Vallestrella. But Luna sides with Elena and takes her through the gateway. They don't realize that Victor and Carla are waiting to sneak in after them.

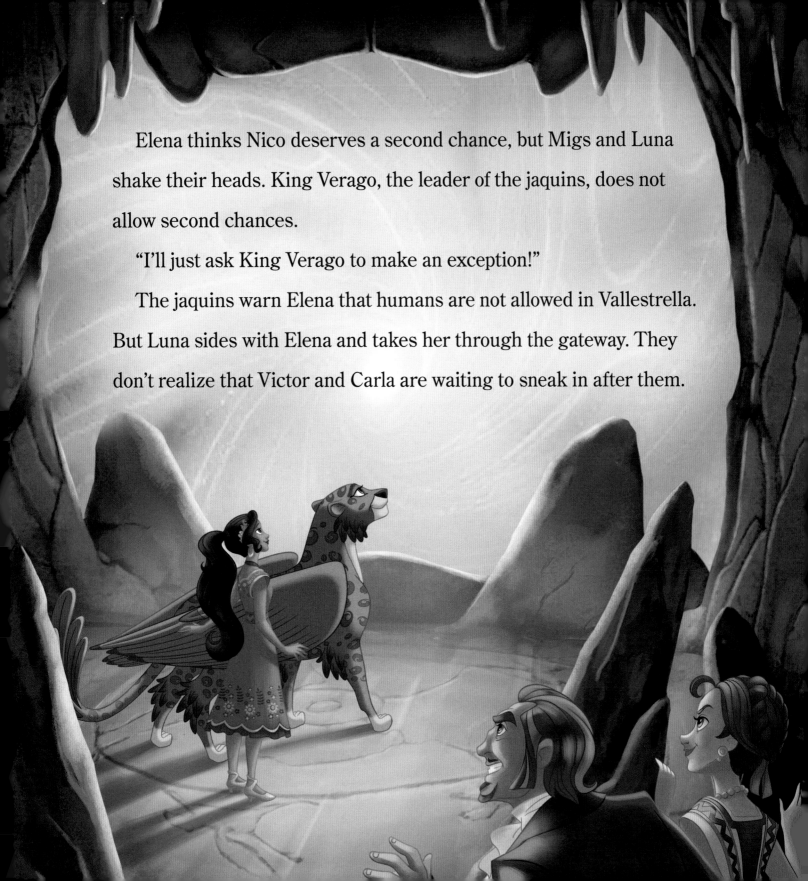

Elena can't believe her eyes. Vallestrella is like nothing she's ever seen! "We're not in Avalor anymore," she marvels.

But there is no time to waste. Elena and Luna head straight for the Palace of the Jaquins and King Verago.

Elena and Luna catch up to Skylar and Nico outside the palace.

Their father's voice booms from inside the palace. "Welcome to Vallestrella, Princess. Now you must go!'

"Ruler to ruler, is it really such a big deal?" asks Elena.

"It is a VERY big deal," Verago growls. He warns her that there is dark magic in Vallestrella, and it is the jaquins' duty to keep it safely locked away.

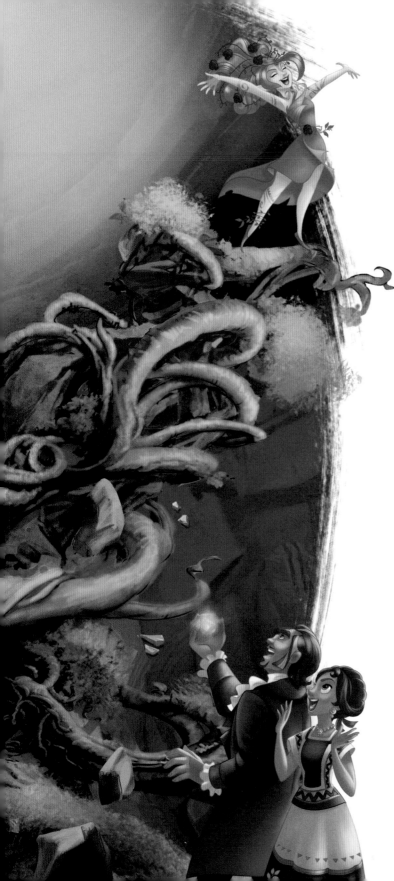

Not far away, Victor and Carla
are trying to release some of the
dark magic. Using an ancient map,
they locate a mysterious cave.
Victor removes a special jewel
from the wall . . . and releases
a wicked forest sprite. Her name is
Marimonda, and she hates cities!
She wants to turn the whole world
into a thick forest. She speaks in silly
rhymes, but her words are cruel.

"Yes, I have no time to waste. To
Avalor I'll go in haste.

I'll visit every ugly town

And use my vines to tear them
down!"

Moments later, two guards enter the palace. "Marimonda has escaped!" one tells the king.

Skylar says only the great sunbird oracle, Quita Moz, would know how to stop her. Elena wants to look for him, but the king says Elena must return to Avalor.

As soon as Verago leaves, Elena asks her friends to help. "My instincts are telling me we have to find that oracle."

Skylar is worried about disobeying his father, but he agrees to help.

Legend says that Quita Moz's nest is on an island in a lake with three mountain peaks above it. They find the island and discover a secret tunnel inside. Elena leads them ahead, lighting the way with her Scepter of Light. The tunnel ends at a mysterious doorway. As Elena approaches, the doorway flies open by itself. Elena tumbles inside, and the door closes behind her!

A strange blue fire burns in the center of the room.

"Welcome," booms a mischievous voice. And then the sunbird rises up behind the blue flames. He peers down at Elena, the blue firelight dancing in his eyes. "I've been expecting you."

"Are you Quita Moz?" asks Elena.

"You better hope so, after coming all this way," says the old sunbird.

"If you're going to run around with that scepter, you need to learn all its powers," Quita Moz says. He teaches her that her scepter can create magical illusions.

Quita Moz hands Elena an enchanted jar. He tells her to trap Marimonda in the jar and bring her back for safekeeping.

"But how do I get her in?" asks Elena.

"That's a good question. Hope you figure it out before you see her. Adios!"

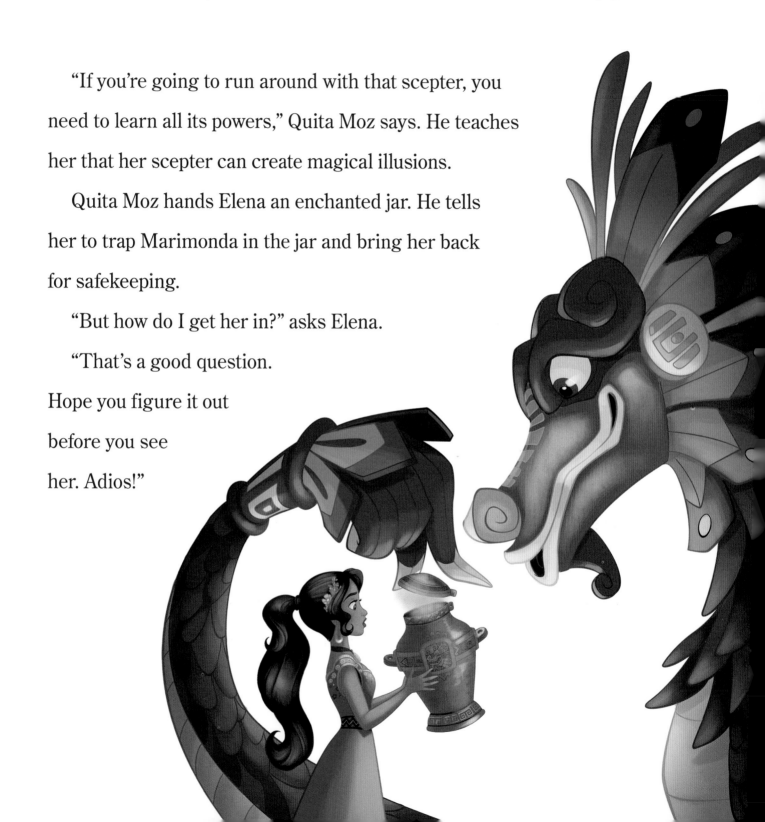

Elena and her jaquin friends race across Vallestrella searching for Marimonda. They need to stop her before she can reach Avalor and destroy its buildings!

Using the new power that Quita Moz taught her, Elena creates an illusion of a house, hoping to lure and capture the forest sprite in the enchanted jar.

It's working! As soon as Marimonda sees the house, she wants to bury it in greenery. She heads toward the illusion, chanting to herself.

"Say farewell to where you dwell."

But before Marimonda is captured, Victor knocks
Elena's scepter out of her hand.

Elena drops to her knees, exhausted from using her scepter. In that
moment, Victor, Carla, and Marimonda escape and head straight to Avalor.

King Vcrago and the other jaquins find Elena. They have to recapture Marimonda. Everyone agrees to join forces, and together they travel to Avalor. When they catch up with Marimonda, she is racing across Avalor, burying buildings in a thicket of vines as she goes. And she's headed for the palace! But Elena has a plan.

The palace guards try to stop Marimonda, but she ties them up in more vines. Even King Verago and the jaquins are no match for her dark magic!

"You can try a trick,

But I'm too quick!"

Marimonda cackles with glee as she prepares to enter the palace. But she gasps in surprise when her foot goes right through the stone step.

"Guess what, Marimonda?" Elena says. "You can be caught after all."

Suddenly, the palace disappears. It was an illusion Elena created! Marimonda fell for the trick. Elena captures her in the enchanted jar.

Elena returns the jar to Quita Moz.

All is safe in Avalor, thanks to Princess Elena. As they celebrate their victory, King Verago proclaims Nico will be a guardian of Avalor. Nico got his second chance—also thanks to Elena!

In the end, Elena doesn't feel as certain that she's got this ruling thing down. But with good advice from the Grand Council and all her friends, she knows she'll be ready for the next challenge.

Mickey and Donald Have a Farm

Mickey has a surprise. "Welcome to the Clubhouse Farm!" he says. Mickey and Donald grow fruits and veggies on the farm. They raise animals, too! The Clubhouse Farm is a very busy place.

All of a sudden, a mighty wind begins to blow. Everything is being blown around—even the animals!

"That wind could wreck the farm," warns Mickey.

He has to shout to be heard over the whooshing wind. But there is another sound—an unusual whirring sound.

"Come on, guys," calls Mickey. "Let's hop in the Clickety-Clack Tractor and find out what's making that strange sound!"

Mickey and the gang follow the whirring sound to their neighbor's farm.

"It's a giant windy-mill!" says Goofy.

"Farmer Pete! What's going on?" asks Mickey.

"Sorry for all the wind," says Pete. "I was using my new windmill to keep the bugs away from my prize petunias."

"Why don't you turn the windy-mill off?" yells Goofy. But Pete doesn't know which lever turns it off.

There are three levers. Goofy remembers that red means stop. He grabs the red lever and pulls.

"The windmill stopped!" Mickey cheers. Mickey and the gang head back to the Clubhouse Farm.

"Thanks, everybody," calls Farmer Pete, as he waved goodbye to his neighbors.

Back at the farm, something is plainly wrong. All the animals are missing.

"They must have blown away like the birdies," says Goofy.

"Come on," says Mickey. "Let's find the animals."

Just then, the friends hear a familiar whinny. But where is the sound coming from? Minnie and Daisy point up. The pony is sitting on top of the silo!

"We've got to help that horsey," says Goofy. "If only she could fly."

Mickey calls Toodles. They decide to use the Blimpy Blazer!

Suddenly, the friends hear another sound. It's the piggies! The piggies are in the chicken coop tower and are ready to come down.

"Uh-oh," says Mickey. "The piggies need a safe place to land!"

Toodles appears in a jiffy with the perfect Mouseketool—a nice soft blanket. Donald and Goofy fold the blanket tight as the piggies glide down the twisty slide.

On the way back to the barn, Mickey hears Clarabelle calling for her lost chickens.

"Oh, cluck-cluck chickens, where can you be?"

Mickey has an idea. "Your chickens love to sing," he says to Clarabelle. "Let's all sing together. I bet the chickens will come out and join in, too."

Before long, Clarabelle's chickens come out of the tall grass. Clarabelle is so happy. "Oh, thank you, Mickey!" she says.

Mickey smiles. "Aw, helping friends is what friends are for!"

Another farm friend needs help, too.

"Cowabunga!" says Goofy. "Mrs. Cow is stuck in that tire like a cork in a bottle!"

"Moo!" says Mrs. Cow as she sways back and forth.

"It's not safe to get too close to a swinging cow," says Mickey. "I think we need a Mouseketool!"

"What if we use the handy fishing pole to catch the tire?" asks Mickey.

"Yeah!" says Goofy. "Then the tire would stop swinging!"

"And the cow, too!" Donald adds. Donald catches the tire and holds it steady. "I did it!" he shouts.

"Okeydoke, Mrs. Cow," Goofy says calmly. "Just wiggle yourself out and . . ." Suddenly, Mrs. Cow pops free and lands right in Goofy's arms!

"Hot dog!" says Mickey. "Now it's back to the barn!" Then, without warning, a clap of thunder surprises everybody! Dark clouds roll across the sky.

"We need to blow away these stormy clouds," says Mickey. "We can use Pete's windmill!"

"But that's what blew away all the animals!" says Goofy.

"Yes," says Mickey. "But now we can use it to blow all the clouds away!"

Mickey tilts Pete's windmill to the sky. "Pull the lever that makes the windmill go," he says.

"Red means 'stop,' so it's not the red lever," Goofy says. "But green means . . ."

"It means 'go'!" shouts Donald as he pulls the green lever. The windmill's powerful blast of air quickly blows the storm clouds away!

Mickey drives the wagon full of animals back to the barn.

"Hooray!" shouts Minnie. "All the animals are back!"

"Goody, goody!" says Daisy.

"Moo-arvelous!" adds Clarabelle.

The farm is saved!

Smitten with a Kitten

O

ne afternoon, Doc introduces her toys to a new friend—a little toy kitten! The kitty's owner donated her to the school's secondhand sale.

"That is the cutie-cutest kitty ever!" Lambie squeals with excitement.

Lambie twirls and says, "If I adopted her as my pet, I would love her and cuddle her and cuddle her some more! Could I adopt the kitty? Pretty pink please?"

Doc says adopting a pet is a super thing to do!

"Ready for your first cuddle?" Lambie says. But the kitten is shy and backs away. Lambie doesn't understand. "Everyone likes my cuddles!" she cries.

Lambie tries to cuddle the kitten again, but the kitty leaps off the bed,

climbs a curtain, and jumps onto Doc's bed canopy!

"Uh-oh!" Stuffy yells. "Cat's on the run! Code nine lives!"

"Come down, kitty. I'll catch you!" Lambie calls. But the kitten jumps off

the canopy and scurries out of sight.

Lambie is heartbroken.

"Maybe she's afraid. It's scary to be in a new house with new toys," Doc explains. Doc says the kitty might not run away if they're very quiet and careful not to frighten her.

Doc and the toys tiptoe to where the kitten is hiding. Doc crouches down, holds out her hand, and gently says, "Heeeeeere, kitty."

When the kitten runs into Doc's arms, Lambie is thrilled!

"Do you think you could give my kitty a checkup now?" she asks.

"You're great at this adoption thing," Doc tells Lambie. "Taking your pet to the vet is a BIG part of being a pet owner. Now let's go get your pet a checkup!"

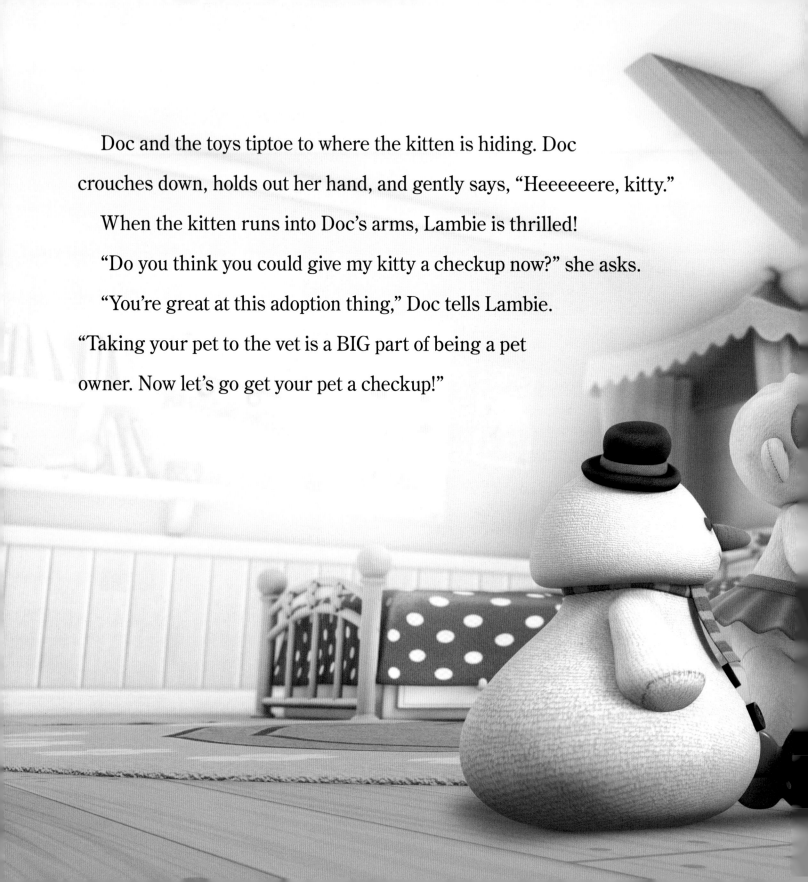

Doc and the toys take the kitten to the Pet Vet clinic for her first checkup.
"We're going to need a brand-spanking-new chart!" says Hallie.

The kitty bats Doc's stethoscope. "She's playful. That's a good sign," Doc
says. Then she listens to the kitten's heartbeat. It sounds strong.

"I bet my kitty has the baa-biggest heart!" Lambie coos.

Doc and the toys take the kitten to the Pet Vet clinic for her first checkup.

"We're going to need a brand-spanking-new chart!" says Hallie.

The kitty bats Doc's stethoscope. "She's playful. That's a good sign," Doc

says. Then she listens to the kitten's heartbeat. It sounds strong.

"I bet my kitty has the baa-biggest heart!" Lambie coos.

Next Hallie takes the kitten's temperature with a thermometer.

"Temperature's normal," Hallie reports.

"Great!" Doc replies. "Now let's get her weight."

Doc puts the kitten on a special veterinarian's scale. But the kitten gets

scared again. She jumps off the scale and onto Stuffy's back.

"Hey, where did the kitty go?" Stuffy asks. "Here, kitty, kitty!" The kitten

lets out a tiny meow.

Doc gently places the kitten on the vet table to check her eyes and ears. When she shines the light from the otoscope on the wall, the kitten bats at the light.

Doc says the kitten is healthy. She just needs a little cleaning up and lots of love!

"Sounds purr-fect," says Lambie. After the kitten has a bubble bath, Doc brushes her fur.

Next it's time for the kitten to get a collar. The tag has Doc's contact information on it in case the kitty ever gets lost.

"We should put her name on it, too," Doc says.

"I haven't even thought about her name," says Lambie. The kitten lets out the softest meow yet.

"How about Whispers?" Lambie suggests. Everyone thinks Whispers is a great name!

"Just one last thing to get ready for our perfect first cuddle!" says Lambie.

She has a purple bow that looks just like hers. But when she tries to put it on

Whispers, the kitten runs and hides.

"She ran away from me again!" Lambie cries.

"I think I know why Whispers keeps running away," says Doc. "She has a case of Skittery-Kitty-itis." Doc explains that when you rescue a pet, it takes time for the pet to get used to a new home.

"Whispers just needs to settle in. She'll come to you when she's ready."

"I'll always be here for her, but what if Whispers doesn't want me?" Lambie asks. "What if she hides from me forever?"

Lambie is so upset she doesn't notice when Whispers comes out of her hiding spot.

"Look, Lambie," says Doc.

Whispers jumps into Lambie's arms and gives her a cuddle and a big PURR.

"I love you, Whispers," Lambie tells her new pet.

Panda Excess

It's another beautiful day full of adorable babies! Pip is looking at their latest delivery photos on his FlyPad. Freddy plays on the slide with a puppy and baby giraffe while they wait for their next delivery. DING! The shift bell rings. It's time!

Pip and Freddy race to the hangar and wait by the conveyor belt. It sends out a closed crate. Freddy wants to say hello to the cuddly baby they're delivering. He opens the lid and . . . KC slams it shut! She tells Pip and Freddy that inside is the most dangerous baby ever! Dangerously cute, that is.

KC shows them the Adorable Meter. "One look into the baby's eyes and you'll fall under her adorable spell, making it impossible to deliver her."

"You can count on us, KC.
We won't open the crate,"
Pip promises.

But Freddy can't help
himself!

It's a baby panda named Precious.

"That sweet face! That new baby smell! That soft fur! You are the most adorable baby ever!"

As Freddy is oohing and aahing over Precious, their eyes meet . . . and he falls under her adorable spell!

Pip says it's time to deliver Precious to her parents, but Freddy holds the baby panda tight. "No, she's way too cute!"

"What am I going to do?" Pip shouts. "Her parents are in the Mile-High Mountain Range, and I can't fly."

KC comes to help. "Koalas are expert climbers," she says.

"Can I lend a paw?" Pip and KC make a plan.

First they have to sneak the bundle of cuteness away from Freddy.

After a few adorable rounds of peekaboo, Freddy and Precious fall asleep in a snuggly pile. Pip replaces Precious with a pillow.

"We did it!" Pip whispers. "Time to get this sleepy little girl to her family."

With Precious snug in KC's baby carrier and Pip giving directions, they begin their journey. Pip and KC have to make sure not to look Precious in the eyes, or they'll fall under her adorable spell!

Precious does not make it easy! She wants to play. KC can't resist the cuteness any longer! She looks down into Precious's eyes.

KC falls under the adorable spell!

"Keep climbing," Pip says. "We have to deliver Precious to her parents!"

But KC is only paying attention to Precious. She lets go of the rope and—PLOP!—the three of them land in a tree.

With KC under the adorable spell, Pip is the only one who can get them up the Mile-High Mountain Range. It's time to suit up.

Pip begins to climb. "Burp!" Precious squeaks out the cutest burp. Pip doesn't dare look down.

"Achoo!" Precious sneezes the cutest sneeze ever! Pip can't resist any longer. He looks down at Precious, and . . .

He falls under the adorable spell!

Pip stops climbing. Now all three of them are stuck on the side of the mountain.

Meanwhile, back at T.O.T.S., Freddy wakes from his nap. "You're not Precious!" he says to the pillow. Freddy pulls out his FlyPad to find the location of his precious Precious.

Instead, he sees photos of parents holding the babies he and Pip have delivered.

"Look at all those mommies and daddies," Freddy says. "They love their babies so much!"

That's when Freddy realizes that if he really loves Precious, he has to get her to her family, because they love her, too.

He breaks the adorable spell! Now he has to find Pip and KC so they can deliver Precious.

Freddy soars over the Mile-High Mountain Range and scoops Pip, KC, and Precious onto his back.

"Freddy to the rescue!" he shouts.

And he files them up, up, up to the safety of a ledge.

Freddy shows Pip and KC the photos of the families they have united. "Precious is the mostest adorable-iest thing I've ever seen," Freddy tells them. "But there's something even more adorable: family. And Precious won't make it to hers without us!"

POOF! The adorable spell is broken!

"Thanks, Freddy!" Pip says to his friend. "You're clear for takeoff!"

Freddy flies them to Precious's home.

Pip, Freddy, and KC

deliver Precious to her parents.

"Mama! Dada!" Precious says when they open the door.

Precious's parents take one look at their new baby girl, and they

immediately fall in love!

"Together," Pip says, "they make the cutest family."

Vampire for President

Vampirina is running for class president! At home, she practices her campaign speech in front of her family.

"That was spooktacular!" says Boris. "You're really gonna knock 'em dead!"

"Oh, Batkins," adds Oxana, "you're the perfect little candidate!"

The next day at school, Vee is hanging campaign posters when she bumps into her best friend, Poppy, hanging her own posters. Both girls are running for class president!

"Oh, no!" they cry.

"We can't run against each other," says Vee.

"What are we going to do?" asks Poppy.

Just then, Mr. Gore, Vee and Poppy's teacher, walks by.

"Looks like we have some excellent candidates for class president this

year," he says. "I think it's great that you're both running."

The girls look at each other. "Really?" asks Poppy doubtfully.

By the time they finish talking with Mr. Gore, Vee and Poppy realize that either of them would make a great class president,

"Whatever happens, we'll always be friends," says Poppy.

"Of course we will," Vee says. "Best friends!"

Vee and Poppy have lots to do before the election—like decorating their booths! Vee strings lights across hers. Meanwhile, at Poppy's booth, kids help themselves to *poppy*-seed muffins!

Mr. Gore stops by and asks Poppy what she would like to do as class president.

Poppy points to the large red and gold banner above her head. "I thought we could use some new school colors," she says.

Later, in class, Mr. Gore interviews the candidates. Vee goes first. "As class president, I'd love to put together a spooktacular haunted house fundraiser," she says. "And we can use the money we raise to build a new playground and take more field trips."

Poppy's up next. She shows off the new T-shirt she designed with a lion on it. "Presenting . . . my idea for our new school mascot!"

Mr. Gore takes a picture of the candidates. The camera's flash goes off!

"Oh, no!" cries Vee. "My battys!"

Poppy throws her arms up to hide Vee. Poppy and Vee run to the printer to get the photo. Luckily, Vee is blocked by Poppy.

"So pictures aren't your thing," says Poppy. "I know you'll be amazing at the next event. Just keep being you."

Vee takes her campaign right to the students. She walks up to some friends in the cafeteria. "As you know, I'm running for class president. I was thinking we could get some new equipment for the playground."

Vee is interrupted by Poppy, who twirls into the cafeteria with her brother, Edgar. She is making a video!

"Do you want new school colors?" Poppy cries. "How about a supercute lion mascot? Let's make our school ahh-mazing!"

"What a bat-tastic idea!" Vee tells Poppy. Then she starts to worry. "Am I supposed to make a campaign video, too?"

"Not at all," says Poppy. "This is just my style." She puts her arm around Vee. "Don't worry. The most important part is tomorrow when we make our big speeches."

Vee and Poppy make plans to practice their speeches together after school. But as Vee heads to the classroom, she overhears Poppy telling their friend Bridget about her speech.

"And that's when the balloons fall! Edgar brings out the T-shirts. And then my song plays!"

"T-shirts? Balloons? A song?" Vee says. "Kids are going to go batty for Poppy." Vee suddenly feels that familiar nervous feelings. She gets the battys.

After school, as Poppy and Bridget wait for Vee in the hallway, Poppy notices some papers on the ground.

"Look!" she says. "It's Vee's speech." The girls read it together.

Poppy and Bridget are impressed. Vee has so many great ideas! They had to do something to help Vee.

246

Meanwhile, back at home, Vampirina tells her family she's decided to drop out of the race.

"What in werewolves are you talking about?" asks Gregoria, Vee's gargoyle friend.

Vee explains that her ideas for the school are just too different. "Poppy knows what human kids like," she says. "I guess I don't."

The next day at school, as Mr. Gore gets ready to introduce the candidates,

Poppy races to the auditorium to give Vee her speech.

"Thanks," says Vee, "but I'm not running for president anymore."

"But your speech is incredible!" cries Poppy. "The class has to hear your ideas."

Mr. Gore introduces Poppy Peepleson as the first candidate for class president.

"Hi," says Poppy. "As president, I wanted to spruce things up with new school colors and a lion mascot. But they won't really help our school." Poppy looks at Vee. "But I know someone who can."

She tells the students about Vee's ideas for a haunted house fundraiser, healthier school lunches, and more field trips.

"Vee is not only my best friend, she's the best candidate for class president. So . . . I'm with Vee!"

Poppy invites Vee up to the stage as the students clap and cheer.

"Wow!" says Vee. "I love my school, and I never would have felt so welcome if it weren't for Poppy."

"So," Poppy says, "will you serve as class president?"

"Absolutely!" cries Vee.

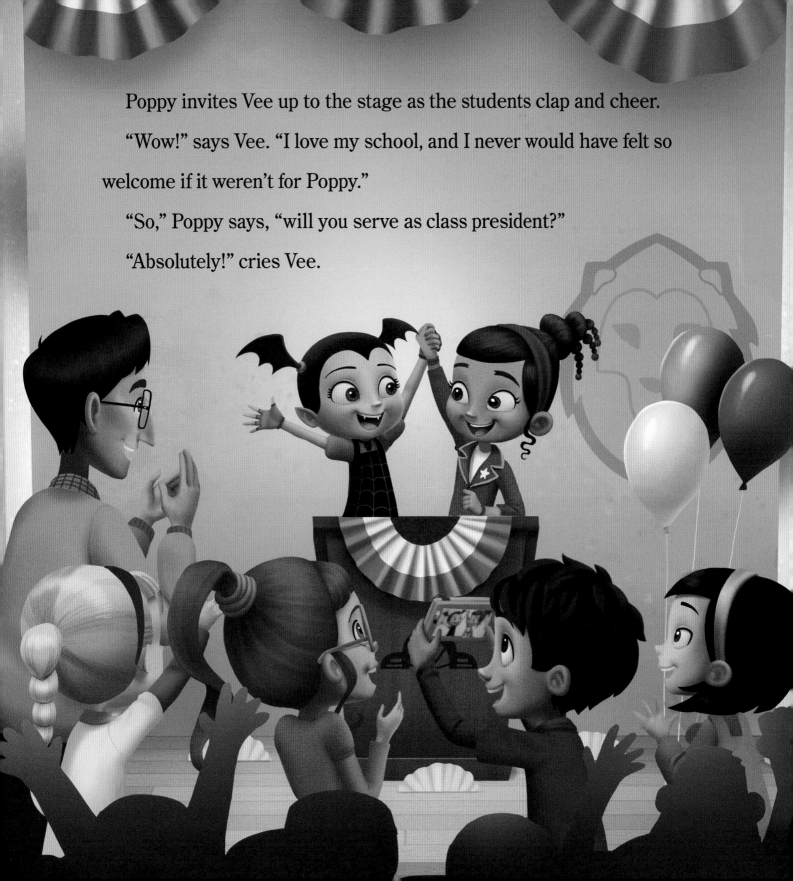

On the day of the haunted house fundraiser, Vee and Poppy are busy selling tickets when Edgar and Bridget come running over.

"This is the best haunted house ever!" Edgar declares.

"All thanks to President Vee," says Poppy.

Vee looks at her friends and smiles. "I guess a vampire really can be president after all."

Hocus-*Bow*-cus

Minnie's Bow-tique is having a magic show! Minnie, Daisy, and Minnie's nieces have been setting up the shop all day in preparation.

"Come see my new line of bows," says Minnie. "They are magical!"

Minnie and Daisy welcome everyone into the shop and point them to their seats. Then the show begins.

"Meet Penguini the magician!" Millie and Melody say in unison. Millie and Melody are his helpers for the show.

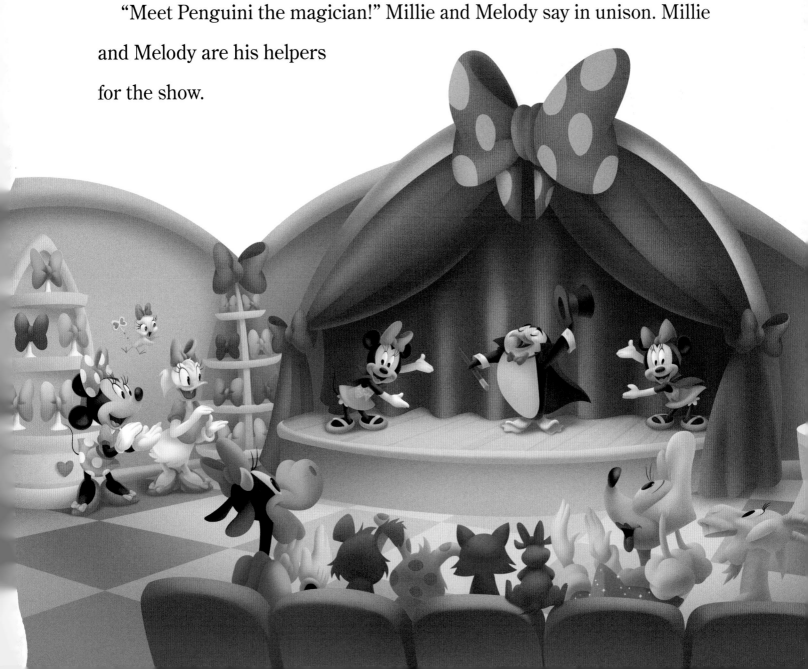

Everyone in the crowd applauds as Penguini takes the stage. Penguini adjusts his hat and then fixes his cape. But something is missing.

"Oh, no!" he cries. "I forgot my lucky bow tie."

"What?" Millie and Melody say as he rushes past them.

"I cannot go on without it!" he says. "I'll be back!" Then he disappears through the door.

After Penguini leaves, the crowd begins to get sleepy and bored. Everyone waits and waits for him to return.

"What should we do?" asks Daisy. Minnie thinks it over.

Suddenly, Minnie has an idea.
She knows how they can save
the magic show.

"Millie, Melody, you know
the tricks, right?" Minnie
asks. "You can do the show!"

"I know the card trick,"
says Millie.

"I know the bunny trick,"
says Melody.

"Let's do it!" the girls cry.

Millie begins the show with the card trick. She pulls Clarabelle from the crowd. She has Clarabelle pick a card.

"Now put it back," Millie says. "I'll say the magic words. Presto chango!"

Cuckoo-Loca springs out of her birdhouse. She has Clarabelle's card!

The crowd is wowed. And the twins are thrilled. The trick worked!

The girls begin to perform more
tricks using the magic words that
Penguini taught them.

"Presto chango!" Millie has a scarf.

"Presto chango!" Melody

has flowers.

"Presto chango!" Daisy has a coin.

"Don't you just love magic?"
Minnie says. Millie and Melody take
a bow as the audience applauds.

"Now for my last trick," Melody says, "I will pull a bunny from this hat!"

She says the magic words. "Presto chango!"

But when they pull the hat up, there is no bunny!

The twins look up at the audience, disappointed there is no bunny. But there is no one in the audience!

"We made everyone disappear! Now we have to get them back," says Millie. She tries to guess the magic word. "Hocus-pocus!"

"Nope," says Melody.

Cuckoo-Loca tries to help. "Abracadabra!" she says.

Cuckoo-Loca seems to have said the magic word. It works! The whole audience magically reappears.

"But they are covered in bows! We need Penguini!" says Daisy.

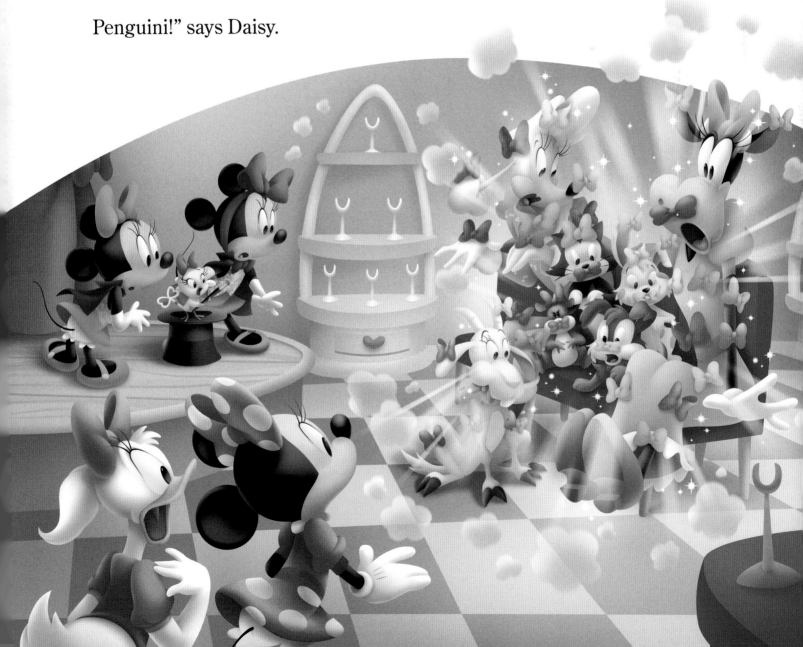

Just then, Penguini runs through the door. "I am here!" he says.

"We need your help," says Minnie.

"I said 'presto chango,'"

says Melody.

"I said 'hocus-pocus,'"

says Millie.

"I said 'abracadabra,'"

says Cuckoo-Loca.

"But the magic words for this trick are . . .

'hocus-*bow*-cus'!" says Penguini.

The trick works! Everything is okay.

"That's much better!" says Minnie.

Millie and Melody go over to Minnie.

"We forgot the magic words," says Millie.

"We got all mixed up," says Melody.

"It's okay!" Minnie says. "We all make mistakes."

"Minnie is right," says Penguini. "It even

happens to the great Penguini."

After the magic show, the members of the audience go shopping.

"Look!" says Daisy. "The Bow-tique is hopping!"

"But where is the bunny now?" says Minnie.

"Hocus-*bow*-cus!" the twins cry. "One bunny coming right up!"

Adopt-a-Palooza

I t's Adopt-a-palooza, the day for pets who need people and people who need pets to meet and become forever families. Bob is volunteering. Bingo, Rolly, and Keia are helping, too!

"This is where Chloe's family met me," Keia says.

Bingo leaps for a ball. But another dog leaps even higher! "Bow to the wow!" Bingo says. "Nice catch!"

"Thanks!" the pup replies.

"I'm Lollie."

Rolly darts over to the puppy playpen. "Baby puppies!" he coos. "They're so cute and tiny."

"I bet every one of these puppies will find a home today," Keia says.

"Except the one that ran away," says Cupcake, pointing to a tunnel. A puppy dug his way out of the playpen so he could chase a squirrel.

"Oh, no!" Rolly cries. If the puppy doesn't get back soon, he'll miss the chance to find a family!

"It looks like we have our mission," Bingo says. "A puppy-finding mission!"

Rolly offers to stay behind to be the puppy-sitter.

MISSION: FIND THE PUP

"We should go talk to the squirrels in the park," Bingo tells Lollie and Keia. "Maybe one of them knows which squirrel the puppy was chasing!"

Bingo and Keia activate their collars. Hang gliders pop out.

"Whoa!" Lollie gasps. "So cool!"

Keia buckles her new friend in tightly. These puppies are ready to fly.

The puppies soar into the treetops, push through piles of acorns, and nudge through nests.

They find plenty of squirrels. But not a single one will talk to them. Every time the puppies get close, the squirrels run away.

Bingo suggests they go talk to the squirrel in Keia's yard. "Why not ask him? He always plays with us!"

"Great idea! Let's go!" Lollie says. Keia leads the way.

In Keia's backyard, they find the squirrel—and the little lost puppy!

"We've got to get you back to the park so you can find a family!" Bingo tells the pup. The puppy starts to follow them, but sees Keia's doghouse and runs inside.

"No! No!" the friends shout. "Stay with us!"

Bingo chases after him. "Sit, puppy, sit!" he yells. Just when Bingo gets

ahold of him, the puppy wiggles away.

"I'll get him, Bingo!" Keia calls.

The puppy rushes into Keia's craft room.

Just when Keia thinks she can grab the puppy, he scampers away.

"I'll get him, Keia!" Lollie calls.

Lollie finds the puppy chowing down on some tasty dog snacks.

"He's here!" Lollie exclaims. "Now how do we get him back to the park?"

"He really likes those snacks," Bingo says. "Maybe he'll follow a trail of treats!"

There's just one problem: Keia doesn't have enough treats to make a trail all the way back to the dog park.

"I wish the squirrel would run back to the dog park," Lollie says. "Then the puppy would chase him again."

"That's brilliant!" Bingo cheers.

"We don't need that squirrel," Keia says. Bingo and Lollie follow Keia to her craft room, where she whips up three squirrel costumes.

"Nice costumes, Keia!" Bingo says. Now the puppy will follow them.

When the puppy sees the three big "squirrels," he starts barking. Bingo,

Lollie, and Keia head to the dog park!

Finally, the little puppy follows them right back to the playpen where he belongs.

"Oh, *now* you fall asleep," Bingo says with a grin.

Just then, a little boy walks up to the playpen with his mother. "Mom, look!" he says. "This puppy has something stuck to his collar. It looks like a cape!" The puppy wakes up and licks the boy's nose.

"Are you a little superhero?" the boy says with a giggle. "Mom, can we adopt this one? We can name him Hero!"

"Okay," his mom agrees. "He does seem sweet."

And that's how little Hero got his name and found his forever home.

MISSION ACCOMPLISHED.

Space Adventure

It's adventure day at the Clubhouse! Mickey and the gang have a treasure map from Professor Von Drake. They're going to the moon, to Mars, to Saturn—and to a mystery planet—to find treasure! The professor says they must find ten Treasure Stars along the way.

Everyone is on board—even Toodles. They count down: ten, nine, eight, seven, six, five, four, three, two, one . . . blastoff!

The gang doesn't know that someone is spying on them. It's Space Pirate Pete! He wants the treasure. Pete has a new helper named Quoodles. He asks her for a tool to stop Mickey's ship. Quoodles brings out milk cartons.

"What good is a milk carton?" asks Pete. "Oh, I see. They all block the rocket!"

"This must be the Milky Way," Goofy says.

"Give up the treasure map!" Space Pirate Pete says.

"No way!" says Mickey. "We need a Mouseketool. Oh, Toodles!"

Toodles brings a Mouseketool. It's a giant cookie! The cookie floats away, and the milk cartons follow it into space. Space Pirate Pete is foiled again! Minnie giggles. "Everyone knows milk goes with cookies."

On the moon, Mickey meets Moon-Man Chip and Moon-Man Dale.

Mickey asks if they have seen any Treasure Stars.

"We see lots of space junk. We put it in our moon locker," they say.

"Then take us to your locker!" says Space Captain Mickey.

Moon-Men Chip and Dale
lead them to their locker.
Goofy opens it.

"I think they need a bigger locker,"
says Goofy. Hot dog! There are
Treasure Stars one, two, and three!

The Treasure Stars fly to the
spaceship and stick on like magic.
"Now we're ready to go to our
next stop," says Mickey. "Mars,
here we come!"

On Mars, Mickey meets Martian Mickey—and Pluto from Pluto! Mickey

asks Martian Mickey if he knows where to find any Treasure Stars.

Martian Mickey says, "They may be in the Star Tree Forest!"

Martian Mickey takes the gang to the Star Tree Forest. "We don't have many trees on Mars, so every tree is a forest," he says. Stars four, five, and six are on the tree. They fly off and go straight to the rocket ship.

Space Pirate Pete has another trick up his sleeve. He pretends to be a little old lady lost in space. The little old lady asks Goofy for a map.

"Goofy, nooooo!" says Donald. But it's too late. Goofy gives Pete the treasure map!

Goofy sure goofed. They've got to get the map back! Mickey, Goofy, and Donald chase Pete around the rings of Saturn, but they can't catch him. Then Mickey falls off the rings and floats away into outer space.

Mickey bumps into space rocks until Pluto rescues him. "Thanks, Pluto," says Mickey.

Pluto and Mickey fly back to Saturn and the ship. On the way, they find the last Treasure Stars: seven, eight, nine, and ten!

Now Mickey and his crew have the map and all ten Treasure Stars. The stars light the way to the mystery planet.

"Hey, that planet looks familiar," says Goofy. "Let's call it Planet Mickey!"

The stars shine on the X that marks the spot. And it's off to Planet Mickey to find the treasure!

But Space Pirate Pete gets to Planet Mickey first and finds the X that marks the treasure spot. Pete has one last trick. He throws out a sticky web. But Quoodles gets stuck in the web.

"I gotta rescue you!" says Pete. "HELP!"

Mickey hears him and comes right away. But Toodles gets stuck, too.

"I have an idea," Mickey says.

"If we want to save Toodles and Quoodles, we have to work together as friends!" says Mickey. Mickey and Pete jump up and down on the arch holding the web. The arch breaks. Toodles and Quoodles are free!

Everyone is happy to meet Quoodles—and to see that Pete has given up his pirate ways. Pluto points to the X. He knows where to dig. Pluto digs up the treasure chest. Inside is Professor Von Drake's remote control. Minnie says, "Push the button, Mickey!"

The ground shakes, and up comes . . .

. . . the Mickey Mouse Space House! What a terrific treasure! Martian Mickey says, "Now when you visit us, you'll have a fun place to play."

"Hot dog!" says Mickey. Everyone does the out-of-this-world Hot-Dog Dance!

As Mickey and the gang head back to their clubhouse on Earth, Martian Mickey waves.

"Thanks for stopping by!"